HE LOVES ME NOT

A NOVEL

NEW YORK TIMES BESTSELLING AUTHOR

DEBORAH BLADON

FIRST ORIGINAL EDITION, MAY 2021

ISBN: 9798743733132
eBook ISBN: 9781926440637

Book & cover design by Wolf & Eagle Media

https://deborahbladon.com

Also by Deborah Bladon

THE OBSESSED SERIES
THE EXPOSED SERIES
THE PULSE SERIES
THE VAIN SERIES
THE RUIN SERIES
IMPULSE
SOLO
THE GONE SERIES
FUSE
THE TRACE SERIES
CHANCE
THE EMBER SERIES
THE RISE SERIES
HAZE
SHIVER
TORN
THE HEAT SERIES
RISK
MELT
THE TENSE DUET
SWEAT
TROUBLEMAKER
WORTH
HUSH
BARE
WISH
SIN
LACE
THIRST
COMPASS
VERSUS
RUTHLESS
BLOOM
RUSH
CATCH
FROSTBITE
XOXO

Chapter 1

Bianca

"The world could do with fewer men." I shove my hand into a plastic bowl filled with peanuts, only for it to topple over. "Screw you."

"Screw me?" A man's voice growls next to me.

It growls. The type of deep and raw sound that enters your ear, but then it crawls down your body lighting up every nerve ending.

I turn because who wouldn't want to see what this guy looks like?

The face outdoes the voice tenfold.

He has dark brown hair that's too long on top to be corporate but stylish enough on the sides to be contemporary.

I look into brown eyes that are a shade lighter than a great espresso.

His nose looks like it was gifted to him courtesy of a Greek god, and his jawline is so sharp that other men must question their masculinity when they're in his presence.

I may be exaggerating, but I've known a guy or two who would hide in a hole after seeing the man sitting on the barstool next to me.

The gray suit he's wearing is next level, as is the silk tie that has thin lines of lilac thread crisscrossing through it.

"I wasn't talking to you," I toss back because I'm not single.

What a waste this encounter is going to be.

"I thought I heard an invitation." He pops a dark brow. He evens that out with a smirk.

Full pink lips and a tongue that I get a hint of when he licks his lower lip only add to his *whatever-the-hell-it-is*. It trumps charisma by miles, and attractive isn't even in the ballpark.

This man could charge money for women to sit and stare at him.

I raise a finger when the bartender approaches, because truth be told, this is not my first time in this questionable establishment.

I have to pick and choose where I show my face in this town.

Manhattan is vast, but my stepfather's reach surpasses that.

I glance at the hands of the man sitting next to me. I tell myself it's because I want to see what he's holding. (A glass half-filled with top-shelf bourbon, from the looks of it.) But, size does matter when it comes to doughnuts and dicks.

If you're going to indulge, satisfaction should be guaranteed.

The suit sitting next to me has large hands.

They are strikingly larger than my current boyfriend's. Kieran's hands are average. They do the job, or they used to.

Some say you can't judge the size of a cock by the owner's hands. I say you can. My research has proven it.

A glass with a little too much vodka and not enough cranberry juice is set just to the left of me. "Thanks, Rolly."

Rolly knows what I like down to the two lime wedges he's propped on the glass's rim.

"I'll add it to your tab, Miss Marks."

Apparently, Rolly has never seen an episode of Dateline. Identifying information in a bar is a no-no. With a discreet shake of my head, I roll my eyes even though I doubt that Rolly will see it.

I'd estimate that the prescription for his eyeglasses dates back to the nineties. He tosses a kiss in my general direction, thrown from his palm because Rolly is a kind soul. He makes a mean drink too and strong. It's very strong.

"Go ahead and put it on my tab." The man next to me leans closer, and I get my first scent of him. I can't tell if it's cologne or just his skin, but it makes me think of his lips in places other than the rim of his glass.

There's no harm in letting him buy me a drink, so I smile. Pushing my long brown hair over my shoulder, I look at him. "Thank you."

He stares into my blue eyes as if I'm going to share my deepest secret with him. "You're welcome, Miss Marks."

Thanks a hell of a lot, Rolly.

"I'm Roman Hawthorne." He extends a hand, and I get a glimpse of an obscenely expensive gold watch peeking out from beneath the sleeve of his suit jacket.

My stepdad would be jealous, which makes me think this man might be even richer than the Marks brood is.

I take his hand for a brief shake. "Miss Marks."

He lets out a chuckle that vibrates through him. "Tit-for-tat, Miss Marks."

My gaze drops to the front of the royal blue blouse I'm wearing. I'd make a comment about my breasts, but there is no need. Mr. Hawthorne has his eyes pinned on them. He'd be getting an eyeful in the form of a black lace bra if this blouse was sheer, but it's not.

"A first name," he says as though it's a question.

I sip on the drink even though I want to down it in one large gulp. I haven't forgotten why I'm here, although the five o-clock shadow on this guy makes me almost forget I have a boyfriend.

The last time Kieran went down on me, he had a beard.

That was weeks ago.

Lately, it's been one minute of foreplay in the form of a swipe of his finger over my clit, three minutes of thrusting before Kieran comes, and ten minutes with my vibrator after I get back to my place.

"I have one," I bounce back.

He laughs, and time in all its infinite wisdom stops. Even Rolly looks in our direction to see where the glorious sound is coming from.

I take another drink.

"Let's start again," he says through a lingering chuckle. "You said something about the world needing fewer men. What was that about?"

"That was about one John Smith."

That is my boss's name, but Roman can't track me down based on that. That's assuming that he'd want to track me down. For all I know, he's in here drowning his sorrows because his girlfriend left him.

I laugh out loud at that.

What woman in her right mind would leave him?

Roman's brows pinch together. "Was that a joke?"

"No," I sigh. "My boss passed me over for a promotion today."

"Bastard," Roman snaps the word off his tongue.

I'd call John worse, and I have, but I did that on the trek here in the sweltering New York City heat.

I'm all cursed out, for now.

"He gave the job to one of his cronies." I edge my manicured, pink-tipped nail along the rim of my glass. "If that's what you call an old friend who has much less experience than me."

"I call it favoritism." Roman finishes his drink. "John Smith made a mistake."

For someone who has no idea what I do for a living, I admire his commitment to taking my side.

"I think it's time to look for a new job," I say half-heartedly.

I've been working at Packton Properties for four years. The senior project manager's job should have been mine. Once John's BFF was put on staff, my chance for any advancement went up in smoke. You'd think that eighty-year-old men would be ready to hang up their hats and hit the retirement path, but not John and Jim.

"If you have a background in law, I'd consider offering you a position with my firm."

That has to be the smoothest humble brag I've ever heard. I don't take the bait because my only experience with the law was a warning for crossing against a light when I was seventeen. I've stayed on the straight and narrow for the past ten years.

I take another sip of my drink, waiting for Roman, the gorgeous but not modest attorney, to ask for my number. My ego hopes he will, even though I can't share it because of Kieran.

I am many things, but I'm not a cheater.

He takes a look at his enviable watch. "It's been an experience, Miss Marks. I hope the employment situation sorts itself out."

"I'll sort it out." I catch his eye one last time. "Thank you again for the drink, Mr. Hawthorne."

"Roman." He taps his fingers on the top of the bar. "It's Roman to you."

He stands. All six-feet-two-inches of him are breathtaking.

I'll never see him again after today, so I take one last, very long look at him.

"Until we meet again," he says, buttoning his suit jacket. "Good day, Miss Marks."

Taking a deep breath, I turn back to my drink and whisper, "You made it a very good day, Mr. Hawthorne."

Chapter 2

Bianca

There are two life rules a woman should never break. Don't go to bed hungry. I mean it - you'll overeat at breakfast. The other is don't let desire take the wheel.

Keep your wits about you at all times.

I could have followed Roman Hawthorne out of Rolly's Pub this afternoon, but I waited the requisite five minutes before I waved goodbye to Rolly. He blew a kiss to the couple taking seats next to me, but I'm sure they appreciated it.

When I got home, I made myself a mocktail because limits are a girl's best friend. Then, I opened my laptop, typed in Roman's name, and ogled everything that popped up on Google.

That amounted to a whole lot of corporate stuff.

Mr. Hawthorne works in estate law and has a partner named Thomas Harrell. Their shared bio speaks of their time at Harvard Law School.

I'm semi-surprised that Roman didn't drop that impressive bombshell on me.

The rest of the information on the website of Hawthorne & Harrell is generic dribble about their mission statement and ode to do well by all who pay them an exorbitant fee to handle their dying wishes.

I'm paraphrasing, but that's the gist of it.

I put my laptop on the coffee table and swallow the mocktail in one gulp.

It does nothing to chase away the buzz running through me.

I'd call Kieran to come here to take care of me, but the subway ride from his apartment in Brooklyn will take longer than our encounter.

I inch a finger up my thigh. Taking this to the bedroom would be the smart thing to do. It's been a long day. I deserve some me time.

That idea is interrupted by a knock at my door.

Kicking off my heels, I stand and adjust my skirt.

Before I'm halfway across my living room, there's another knock. "I'm coming."

This is a doorman building on Madison Avenue. Any visitors are supposed to check in with the front desk, but when Lester is on duty, he almost always escorts them up.

For a doorman, he's making bank on tips.

He knows I'll slip him a few bills when I open the door to find any of my friends on the other side.

Just as a series of fast-paced knocks start, I swing it open. It's my neighbor from 3A. I live in B, no one is currently renting C, and D is undergoing a massive renovation.

"Hi, Mrs. Fields." I smile. "How are you?"

"Hungry."

It's more like hangry judging by the scowl on her face, but I'll play along. "You haven't eaten yet?"

I'd laugh if anyone asked me that right now. It's not even seven. I don't start thinking about what I'm craving until at least eight, and if food hits my stomach by nine, I'm happy.

"My food is missing." She brushes past me and enters my foyer. "Do you mind if I check around for it?"

I should be offended that she thinks I stole her dinner, but I'm not. I'm responsible for most things that go wrong in her life. I don't take that personally, or I haven't since I found out that none of her grandchildren visit her.

"Let me call Lester and see if there's been a mix-up."

I don't need to be a detective to solve the case of the missing fish sticks. Lester is holding Mrs. Fields's food hostage until she rides the elevator down to the lobby to search for it. Once she pays the ransom of a hefty tip, he'll conveniently hand it to her with the explanation that he was just about to bring it to her apartment.

I tap the button on my phone to call Lester directly.

"Hello, Miss Marks. To what do I owe the pleasure?"

I turn my back and lower my voice, so Mrs. Fields isn't privy to what I'm about to say. "Stop playing games, Lester. Bring Mrs. Fields's food up here now."

He clears his throat. "Is she looking for it?"

"She's starving," I stress. "Do you want to be personally responsible for her passing out?"

"I'm not sure what you mean."

I hold the upper hand. I rarely play it, but today Lester has left me no choice.

"Do I need to call Sabrina to get her involved?"

He lets out an audible gulp. "I'll rush the food right up, Miss Marks."

"Bring it to my apartment."

"I'm on my way," he declares before he ends the call.

I turn to give Mrs. Fields the good news, but she's helped herself to my laptop. "Who is this handsome fellow?"

I don't need to look at where her finger is pointed. "He's a lawyer."

"You'd do well to steer clear of lawyers," she warns as she places my laptop back on the table. "They are the best liars in the world."

Since I'll never see Roman Hawthorne again, I nod. "I'll take that advice to heart."

Her face softens. This is all she needed. She just wanted her dinner and someone to listen to her wisdom.

I steer her toward my apartment door with a hand on her back. "Lester is on his way up with your dinner."

"It was just delivered?"

The knock at the door saves me. "Here it is now."

I snatch the bag from Lester's hands as soon as the door is opened. After a brisk "*thank you*," I slam it shut.

Mrs. Fields doesn't notice because she's too enamored with whatever is in the white paper bag that smells delicious.

"What do you have there?" I crane my neck to get a better look.

"Salmon with olives and artichokes." She digs a hand in the bag. "There is also a rice dish. I can't recall the name, but they always know what I like when I call to order."

"From where?" I question because, in a few hours, this may be my dinner too. I'll make an in-person visit so I can enjoy my meal with a glass of white wine. I'll drag my sister, Viviana, with me since I haven't seen her in almost two weeks.

"Nova."

Dammit.

It takes months to get a table there.

I may have to settle for take-out for dinner tonight and a text to Vivi telling her that our sister bonding time will have to wait.

"I'll go home and enjoy this." She grabs the door handle. "Remember what I said about lawyers, Bianca. You can't trust them. They may look nice, but the devil is hiding under the suit."

"No lawyers for me," I say honestly because Kieran works on Wall Street.

He chases after the almighty dollar for a high. He has that in common with my stepfather.

The door opens to the sight of Lester pacing in front of the bank of elevators.

I stand guard while Mrs. Fields heads back to her apartment. Once her door is closed, Lester glances in my direction.

"Miss Marks, if I can have a word."

"I won't say anything to Sabrina this time," I stress my cousin's name. "Don't play games with Mrs. Fields again."

He stabs the elevator call button with his index finger at least six times. "I won't. Thank you, Miss."

Once he boards the lift, I turn and head back into my apartment.

My eye catches on the open laptop on my coffee table and the headshot of Roman Hawthorne.

Our brief encounter today is proof that Manhattan is home to some of the most breathtakingly handsome men in the country. It's also home to my boyfriend.

I pick up the laptop, exit the page, and clear my search history.

By tomorrow morning, Roman will be nothing but a memory to me.

Chapter 3

Bianca

"Are you still in mourning?" Paige Barben asks from where she's seated behind her desk.

We met over two years ago when she came to work for Packton Properties. She heads up the marketing department. I'm still holding down my position as an assistant project manager. Since I was passed over for the promotion, I've made a few inquiries at other real estate development companies, but so far, I've heard nothing back.

Biting back a smile, I tilt my head. "Why would you ask me that?"

"You've worn a little black dress to work for days." She looks at the bright yellow ensemble she has on. "I happen to know that your spring wardrobe is killer. You're hiding that away because you're trying to make a point."

"You're very perceptive." I tap her on the top of her head as I breeze past her.

She runs a hand through her blonde hair. "Mr. Smith hasn't noticed. He doesn't care what you wear as long as you're decent."

Until an hour ago, I would have agreed with her, but John has been eyeing me up through the glass wall of his office since he arrived at work. He was uncharacteristically late. He greeted me with a wave and a smile.

Most days, I get nothing from him, so something is up today.

"Bianca, I need to see you in my office."

Paige's brown eyes widen when she realizes that our boss just called out to me through the office PA system.

We have phones, but John likes to kick it old-school style.

If pagers make a comeback, he has at least a dozen stored in a cardboard box in the supply room.

I look in the direction of his office to find him on his feet. His suit jacket is on, so he means business. John is typically dressed in one of his stained white button-down shirts and a tie in a ghastly shade of brown.

Today the tie is light blue.

I smooth my hands over the skirt of my black dress. This one has lace at the collar and a cute thin leather belt around my waist. My black shoes have three-inch heels.

I'm five-four, so whenever possible, I try to get closer to eye level with the people I'm talking to.

"Give him hell, Bianca," Paige whispers as I take the first step toward our boss's office.

I toss a look over my shoulder in her direction. "I will. I have nothing to lose at this point."

That's a lie. I have a job to lose. It's not the one I want, but it's the one I have at the moment. The alternative is going to work for my stepfather. That's never going to happen.

***

"Have a seat." John gestures toward one of the white leather chairs that face his massive desk.

I settle into the middle one. I always do when I'm summoned in here. The first time that happened, I asked my boss why he has three chairs facing his desk instead of two. He answered that he likes odd things.

One glance around his office confirms that. For one of the most successful real estate developers in Manhattan, John's office decor looks like it was stolen from a circus tent.

There are clown figurines everywhere. A portrait of a monkey playing cymbals hangs on the wall behind his desk, and a life-sized bearded mannequin in a red coat with tails and a top hat stands in the corner. He's the ringmaster, or so John says.

I cross my legs. "How are you today?"

Pleasantries are born and bred into my blood. My dad taught me to mind my please and thank yous before he died. I always do as a way to honor him.

John nervously picks at a white spot on his tie. "I'm fine."

He's not. He's growing increasingly frustrated as he tries to grab whatever that is. It's proving to be an impossible task, judging by the way he keeps near missing it.

"I'm fine," he repeats. "It's been quite the day."

"There's still time to turn it around," I volley back to lighten his mood.

He ignores me because he's still on a mission to win his battle with the white spot on his tie.

"Maybe that's a spot of cream?" I offer because I've worked for the man long enough to know that what's in his coffee cup doesn't always end up where it should.

He licks the pad of his thumb before rubbing it over the silk tie. I watch as the white spot disappears, only to be replaced with a saliva smudge.

"It must have happened when I was having coffee this morning." He straightens the tie. "It was an important meeting. I may have been nervous."

I'd bet all the money in my bank account that he was nervous since he's practically shaking in his shoes right now.

Unsure of why I'm here, I try to get this meeting back on track. "Is there something I can help you with?"

He scrubs at the back of his neck. "I realize that I made a mistake, Bianca."

I fold my hands in my lap. I don't want to assume anything, but I'm hoping he's about to tell me he picked the wrong person for the promotion.

Jim took a two-hour nap yesterday afternoon on the bench in reception. The only thing he's mastering as the new senior project manager is the senior part.

The fact that he's been retired for the past twenty years may be the reason he hasn't found his stride yet. After all, he's only been working here for a week.

"What mistake is that, John?" I plant a smile on my face.

He moves to stand in front of his desk. "You've worked hard since I hired you."

I nod because *damn right, I have.*

"Any developer in this city would be lucky to have you on the payroll."

"Thank you."

A compliment always needs to be acknowledged, especially if the person offering it signs your paycheck.

"I got word that one of my competitors is interested in you."

I do everything in my power not to jump up, dance in a circle, and ask who it is.

"I can't let anyone steal you away." John leans his hip against his desk. "I want you to take on the role of our senior project manager."

I let go and dart to my feet. I reserve the dancing for later when I'm at home.

John cracks a half-smile. "I haven't broken the news to Jim yet, so don't tell anyone."

This feels like a first-grade secret, but I'm on board. I place my index finger over my lips. "I'll stay quiet until you tell him."

Sweat peppers his forehead. "This may be the end of a lifelong friendship, but I have no choice. What else was I supposed to do? I had to give you the job or else."

I was hoping for a few complimentary words about my outstanding ability and his confidence in the great work I've done in the past.

This hits different, so I ask. "Or else what?"

He laughs that off in a nervous cackle. "Oh, nothing, Bianca. All I meant is that you're the future of this company, and…no…you're going to take this company to great places in the future. Your youth and experience, and talent are great. Just know that you are a young, talented, and experienced woman who will do great things."

Either this guy is a spot-on body double for my boss, or he just fumbled his way through a horribly memorized speech.

"Is everything all right, John?" I ask, wondering if my stepfather decided to stick his nose where it doesn't belong again.

He wipes the bottom of his tie over his brow, leaving another stain. "Everything is A-OK. I need to go to reception to wake up Jim and give him the bad news. Wish me luck."

My gaze trails him as he sprints out of his office. "Good luck, boss."

He stops to turn and look at me. "Why don't you take the rest of the day off to celebrate? Grab a drink. You deserve it."

I smile. "I'm going to do that."

I will, right after I have a word with Thurston Marks.

Chapter 4

Bianca

"Your stepdaddy stepped out for the rest of the day."

I cringe, wishing Thurston's secretary could see the expression on my face. "Don't call him that, Shirlene."

She laughs on the other end of the phone before she lets out a stuttered cough. "Why not? That's who he is to you."

Legally, he's more than that. Thurston Marks adopted me right after he married my mom. I didn't want it to happen. I was twelve. My mom was my legal guardian, and she decided that she wanted her new husband to be our new father.

Viviana was ten. She went along with it happily.

I fought the good fight with a ten-hour hunger strike and a neon pink sign taped to my bedroom door with the words *I'm not a Marks* written on it.

Even my bouts of crying didn't help my cause.

My mother signed the adoption papers. Thurston did too, and I went back to school after my seventh-grade winter break with a new surname, an older stepbrother, and no desire to answer any of the questions my friends had for me.

I've grown fond of Thurston over the years, and although I'll never call him dad, I've kept his surname. I've done it more to placate my mother. Since she fought her way through a stage two ovarian cancer diagnosis, I do what I can to make her happy.

"Was he in the office this morning?" I ask Shirlene as I wait for the light, signaling that it's safe to cross the street.

"Bright and early," she chirps. "He got here shortly after seven to do some business with London. He was stuck in meetings, and after that, he went to meet your mother uptown for lunch."

"He didn't leave to have coffee with anyone?"

A slight sigh is followed by a curt, "Nope."

I'm not getting anywhere with Shirlene. I need to see Thurston face-to-face. If he persuaded John to give me the promotion, I have to remind him to keep his nose out of my business.

"Is he at home?" I start the trek across the street with at least twenty other pedestrians all headed somewhere this early afternoon.

"Nope," she answers again with less hesitation this time. "They're going to a matinee on Broadway. It's that musical they've wanted to see all month."

Of course, it is. Thurston will do anything that's asked of him as long as my mom is the person making the request.

"I'll find him later." I smile at a woman passing me.

"Works for me," Shirlene says. "Tell your dad I'll see him in the morning."

She ends the call before I can tell her that I wish I could do that. My dad has been gone for a long time. Every night I fall asleep wishing I could see his face in the morning. That wish will never come true.

***

Cursing under my breath, I shove my phone into my purse. Kieran didn't pick up. I tried to call him twice, but both calls went straight to voicemail. That's a sure sign that he's silenced his phone.

He only does that when he's in one of his "*critical conferences,*" as he calls them. His colleagues refer to them as client meetings, but Kieran eats up drama like it's dessert. It fuels him. He tells me it makes him a better man. I disagree. I think it makes him anxious and unreliable.

I didn't bother leaving a message. I want to hear what I hope will be excitement in his voice when I tell him I landed my dream job.

We've never admitted it to one another, but it's always felt as though Kieran and I are in a silent battle to win the career race.

The last time we compared salaries and perks, he was a step ahead of me. I know, for certain, with this promotion, that I'll take the lead.

I swing open the door to Rolly's Pub because I'm taking my boss's advice to grab a drink. It's early, but it's not every day a dream comes to fruition.

As soon as I step inside the dimly lit pub, my gaze lands on the back of a man sitting at the bar.

I only got a brief glimpse of Roman Hawthorne's back last week, but the expensive suit jacket covering the broad shoulders of the man I'm looking at is familiar.

Lady Luck is definitely shining her bright light on me today.

Before I can approach him, he's turned in his seat.

A smile glides over his devilishly full lips. "Miss Marks."

"Mr. Hawthorne," I say as I step closer.

"Roman," he corrects me. He stands and gestures to the empty barstool next to him. It's the same one I was sitting on when we met. "Please, join me."

I see no reason not to.

I smooth my hands over the skirt of my dress and situate myself so I'm semi-facing him. This skirt is a bit too short for barstools, so I tug at the hem. It settles just above my knees which is exactly where Roman's gaze is.

"Are you drinking the usual?" he asks as he takes his seat. "A vodka and cranberry with two lime slices?"

That shouldn't impress me, but it does since Kieran has never remembered my preferred drink.

"That's what I'm here for," I say, even though if this is Roman's regular mid-day haunt, I may need to drop by more often.

I motion to Rolly to bring me a drink. He tilts his chin in what I hope is a gesture of acknowledgment.

"Did you sort out that job situation?" Roman asks.

My gaze drops to his mouth as he takes a small sip from the glass in front of him. It's almost half-full. I can't tell if that's because he ordered it straight or if he's been in here nursing it for some time.

"I got the promotion I was hoping for."

Roman's gaze roams my face. "That's good news."

"Great news." I smile. "I deserved it."

That's not boasting. It's a fact. I still need to sit down with Thurston to see if he had a hand in John's sudden change of heart. My stepfather has skills when it comes to getting what he wants for himself and those around him. He can't lie, though, at least not to me.

If I look him in the eye and ask him whether he convinced John to give me the job, I'll know the truth.

Even if he did pull some strings or a skeleton out of John's closet that he held over his head, I'm going to do whatever it takes to prove that I'm worthy of the job.

Rolly sets my drink on a paper napkin just to the right of where I'm sitting. I turn to him. "Thanks, Rolly."

"It's my pleasure, Miss Marks."

I smile at him, but he's already headed in the direction of a couple sitting at the far corner of the bar. Their heads are bowed in a hushed discussion.

Roman lifts his glass in the air. "A toast is in order, Miss Marks."

I don't offer my first name even though I'd love to hear it roll off his tongue.

I raise my glass.

"To promotions and chance meetings in bars," he says before he tips his glass to touch the side of mine.

I sip from my drink, trying not to grimace when I realize how strong it is. All of my plans for today may be pushed aside for a mid-day nap if I polish off every last drop of this concoction.

The buzzing of a phone drops Roman's gaze to the front of his dark gray suit jacket. "A man's work is never done."

I take another swallow of my heavy on the vodka drink as I watch his brow furrow when he glances at the phone's screen.

When he lifts his head to look at me, frustration mars his expression. "Duty calls."

Disappointment tugs at me. My drinking partner is about to leave.

Sliding a few bills out of his wallet, he pushes to stand. "If something brings you back this way next Tuesday at the same time, you'll find me here."

Nothing should bring me back. I have a boyfriend. I can't forget that. This is where I should mention that to the tall, handsome, almost stranger.

"Congratulations on the promotion, Miss Marks," he says as he leans down, so his lips are within an inch from my cheek. "Perhaps at some point, I'll be able to demonstrate my favorite way to celebrate."

When he pulls back, our eyes lock, and his unsaid words speak volumes as he drops his gaze to my breasts and then my legs.

I don't comment because of Kieran.

Roman walks away. This time I don't turn to watch him go. Instead, I swallow the drink in front of me in one gulp, hoping it will chase away the urge I have to follow him.

Chapter 5

Bianca

"Blanche? Is that you?"

I tear my phone away from my ear and look at the screen. It says Mortegue Plumbing and Heating. Since all my pipes are in order, I shake my head. "You have the wrong number."

I shouldn't have answered my phone when it started ringing, but I didn't check the incoming caller's name when I was headed out of Rolly's Pub. Now, I'm standing in the afternoon heat on a Manhattan sidewalk, feeling the effects of that strong-as-hell drink Rolly whipped up for me.

"No, not Blanche," the man on the other end of the call scoffs. "It's Bianca, right? My wife's handwriting looks like a squirrel got ahold of a pencil."

What the hell? Am I in the throes of a bad vodka reaction?

"What did you say?"

"I got your number from Kieran Ratchford," he explains. "My next stop is his apartment. He's got a backed-up sink drain, and he's supposed to let me in to fix it. If he didn't pick up, I was told to call you."

It was romantic when Kieran handed me an extra set of keys to his apartment a couple of months ago. I haven't used them because he's always been there when I've arrived, but today I'll do a good deed and help him out.

"I'm in Manhattan. I'll hop on the subway."

"Works for me," the plumber says. "It'll give me time to grab a sandwich. I'll see you soon, Bianca."

"Soon," I repeat back.

Heading toward the nearest subway stop, I give my head a shake. I need to sober up, or I could take a mid-day nap in Kieran's bed.

I'm sure he'll appreciate finding me as a surprise after he deals with whatever critical conference is keeping him from answering his phone.

***

I should feel devastated.

I don't.

I'm relieved in some way, disappointed in another, and angry that I wasted my time on a man who is cowardly enough to cheat on me with his assistant.

I stand at the entrance to Kieran's bedroom with Garen, the plumber, breathing heavily over my shoulder.

Kieran and his blonde-haired assistant, Ulla, are going at it missionary style. The way her head is pounding into the headboard is concerning. I didn't think Kieran had it in him to cause a cockcussion.

It's a term I heard way back in high school after I told my bestie about my first time. She tapped me on the forehead and said I was cockcussed because the guy jackhammered me into his wooden headboard. My head took a beating the day my virginity was lost. The rest of me got a warm buzz, but nothing else.

That same selfish guy gave me a headache a week later when I told him I wanted to blow him. He slid his dick between my lips and thrust his way to an orgasm as my head, once again, pounded out a beat on his headboard.

It was my second cockcussion and my last time with him.

I glance over my shoulder at Garen. All he gives me is a smirk and a half-shrug. Clearing my throat, I tap my hand against the doorjamb. "Kieran!"

The sound of the headboard banging against the wall drowns me out.

Ulla's whimpers aren't helping. Neither is the grunts coming from my soon-to-be-ex-boyfriend.

I drop my gaze to the floor because I don't want this mental image to imprint itself on my memory forever.

I pound my fist against the doorjamb. "Kieran! What the hell?"

Nothing.

The headboard keeps hitting the wall. Kieran continues his relentless thrusting, and Ulla screams something in what I think is Swedish, but that's directed at her boss, not me.

"Dude!" Garen yells. "Your girl is right here, man! Knock it off!"

Finally, Ulla and Kieran turn to look at us. They break apart immediately with her scurrying across the bed to grab a blanket to cover her body with.

The look of horror on her face is obvious. Frustration is all I see in Kieran's expression.

Is he pissed that he didn't get off?

I toss the keys he gave me on the bed, narrowly missing his now deflating penis. "I'm out of here."

Fortunately, I never left a thing at this place. I turn and maneuver my way around Garen, who is still planted firmly in the spot he's been standing in since we wandered down the hallway together after hearing the sound of the persistent thumping coming from the bedroom.

"Bianca, wait!" Kieran calls out. "Just a minute."

I take slow steps toward the apartment door. I know this conversation is inevitable, so I want to have it now. When I walk out of here, this chapter of my life needs to be over.

I turn as I hear his footsteps on the floor behind me.

He's wearing gray sweatpants and a frown. His blond hair is a mess, and red lipstick stains his cheeks in smudged kiss marks.

"Let me explain, B."

I've told him repeatedly not to call me that, but he's never listened.

"Bianca," I correct him. "You know I hate when you call me anything but my name."

His gaze trails over my face. "I'm sorry."

I can tell that he is. I see it in his eyes and the way he's resisting the urge to reach out to me.

"It meant nothing," he says the standard line that people toss out when they want you to sweep their infidelity under the rug. "It was a one time thing."

I sense that he's lying, but it doesn't matter. He cheated. Whether it happened once or a hundred times is inconsequential.

"We've never said I love you to each other," I point out softly. "Did you ever love me?"

"Did you ever love me?" he tosses my question back at me as he crosses his arms over his chest.

He's gone from guilt mode to defense mode in the blink of an eye.

I answer honestly because I won't walk out of here regretting anything I've done or said to him. "No."

He steps back. "You didn't?"

I shake my head. "I cared about you. We had fun."

Nodding, he rubs a hand over the back of his neck. "It was fun."

I grab hold of the strap of the purse slung over my shoulder. "I thought you were a better man than this. If you checked out of our relationship, I deserved to know that. I shouldn't have found out like this."

His gaze darts over his shoulder. "It's a one time thing. I had a critical conference that went to hell. Ulla offered to console me. We ended up here. None of this was planned."

Excuses won't change a thing.

If I were more invested in this, I would be on the floor in a puddle of my tears, cradling my broken heart.

"I'm going to go." I gesture toward his door.

"I'll call you in a few days, B."

"Don't."

He nods. "Understood."

We leave it at that. I thank fate as I step out of his apartment and shut the door behind me.

I lost a cheating boyfriend and landed the job I wanted today.

Life is looking up.

Chapter 6

Bianca

"If I'm totally honest, I should have walked away from Kieran weeks ago," I confess to my sister. "We got along great in the beginning, but then the spark fizzled."

Vivi drags a hand through her shoulder-length brown hair. "You met Kieran on a blind date a few months ago, Bianca. You're the one who told me that those relationships never work out long-term. You just proved your own point."

I hate when my younger sister throws my words back in my face. "What's going on with you? Have you met anyone lately?"

The scowl she gives me is the only answer I'll get to that question.

"When are mom and Thurston supposed to get here?" I glance at the entrance to the restaurant that Vivi chose.

Sérénité serves French cuisine, which happens to be my sister's favorite. I would have thought she'd pick something I adored for this celebratory meal.

It was Vivi's idea to break out the bubbly and our stepfather's credit card for this mini family reunion. She's eager to toast to the fact that I dumped Kieran. She's assured me she won't spill the beans to our mom and Thurston tonight. I'll tell them when the time is right.

I left out all the details of why I pulled the plug on the relationship when I told Vivi it was over. I don't want to recount what I saw this afternoon to anyone. I hoped that the shower I took when I got home would wash the mental image of my boyfriend fucking another woman from my mind, but it didn't.

Time will do that, and a glass of wine tonight will help.

"They'll be here soon," Vivi reassures me with a hand on my arm. "They're excited to see you. You've been so busy lately."

She has been too.

My sister works as an event planner at Howerton House. It's the premier venue in Manhattan for luxury weddings, conferences, and galas.

She loves her job almost as much as I love mine.

I haven't told Vivi that I got the promotion. I want to find a moment alone with my stepfather to discuss his part in that before I make a grand announcement.

My sister jumps to her feet when she sees our mom and Thurston on the approach. My mom, Angela Marks, is dressed as she always is in a pantsuit. Today it's a soft lilac that's a shade lighter than the dress that Vivi is wearing.

Thurston's three-piece suit is dark blue. It's his signature look, along with the bowtie around his neck and his perfectly groomed gray hair.

Since I'm wearing a red sheath dress she bought for me, I get a nod of approval from my mother. Sleek and elegant are two of her favorite words. She wasn't able to indulge in her love for designer brands before she married Thurston. Now, she takes full advantage of his generosity.

"Beauties," Thurston says as he takes Vivi for a hug before he steps closer to pull me into his chest. "How are my girls?"

I glance at my mother. A broad smile lights up her face.

That's enough for me. It's always been since my dad died. Her hugs became less plentiful after he was buried. Her goodnight kisses disappeared. She wove a cocoon around herself that only Thurston has been able to break through.

"Let's sit." Thurston gestures to my mom. "Vivi can tell us why we're gathered here together."

"Surprise!" My sister screams in my ear as we all take our seats. "Bianca got promoted today."

Well, damn.

I look at Thurston, but there's not an ounce of shock in his expression. I'd call it smug satisfaction. My mother, on the other hand, is clapping her hands in excitement.

I turn to look at Vivi. "How did you know?"

Her blue eyes wander my face, trying to find a hint to how I feel. "Paige told me."

I should have seen that coming. They met last month when the three of us had lunch. Paige and Vivi hit it off. I didn't realize they kept in touch, but my sister makes friends with everyone she meets, so this isn't shocking.

Thurston calls over the waiter, who has been hovering a few feet away from us. My stepdad orders a bottle of his favorite champagne for the table. It's the same champagne he popped open on my twenty-first birthday, and the day Vivi was hired at Howerton House.

Our special occasions have always been as important to him as his son Grayson's are. Grayson is a professor at NYU and an award-winning poet. When my mom married Thurston, Grayson was twenty-one and in college.

The waiter departs with a smile on his face. Thurston's been here before. The staff knows that he tips incredibly well.

"John made the right decision." Thurston beams. "You're going to excel, Bianca. I'm confident you'll do well."

I catch his eye. I tilt my head and raise a brow. "Did you speak to John today?"

Holding my gaze, he nods. "He came to me because he had heard that Hudgins Developments were interested in you."

I had reached out to a contact I have there a few days ago to see if there were any available positions. Hudgins isn't near the top of my list of dream employers, but I was looking for a way out of Packton when John handed the promotion to Jim.

Reaching for my mom's hand, Thurston goes on, "John confided in me that he recognized the mistake he'd made in hiring Jim. He was concerned that you were about to resign."

Thurston owns one of the most successful media conglomerates in the world. He developed an interest in real estate investing a decade ago. That resulted in him partnering up with John on a few projects. Their business relationship has sometimes muddied the waters when it comes to my job, but the past couple of years, I've proven my worth to John beyond my ties to the Marks fortune.

I sit silently while the waiter arrives with the champagne. Thurston asks him to give us a minute before the bottle is uncorked.

Once he's out of earshot, Thurston looks at me again. "I told John to speak to you about the promotion. I also explained that he was damn lucky to have you because you will take his company to great places in the future. You have youth, experience, and talent beyond measure. You're a young woman who is going to do great things."

My mom and Vivi let out a collective sigh.

I hold back a smile. John's rambling speech suddenly makes sense. There is one last thing I need clarification on. This seems like the perfect time to bring it up.

"John said he had to give me the job or else," I say. "What's the '*or else*,' Thurston?"

He winks. "I may have said that I was reconsidering my position on the penthouse at the Fifth Avenue project."

There it is. It's the thinly veiled threat wrapped into a discussion about my future.

"You didn't say that." My mom playfully swats her husband on the shoulder. "You know that I've already started ordering furniture for the main room. They're custom pieces, dear. I can't cancel them."

He gathers my mom's hand into his to place a kiss on her palm. "That's your dream home, Angie. I promise we'll live the rest of our lives there. I brought it up to make sure John understood how much the Marks family has done for his business. The least he can do is return the favor by helping our Bianca."

When Thurston first approached me about purchasing the penthouse of the building currently under construction on Fifth Avenue, I scoffed. He persisted, and when he signed the contract, I was given a bonus even though I'm not a sales agent.

The same thing happened when Grayson bought a condo on East Seventy-Eighth Street. John saw to it that I was compensated for the sale. My only part in that deal was taking a stroll with my stepbrother past the site before the contractor had broken ground.

"You're going to kick ass on this job, Bianca." Vivi curls a lock of my hair behind my ear. "It'll help you get over Kieran because you'll be even busier than you normally are."

I toss her a look that says *thanks-a-hell-of-a-lot.*

"Oh no." My mom's hand darts to the middle of her chest. "What happened with you and Kieran?"

"We broke up," I say succinctly.

"Why?" she presses. "He comes from a good family, Bianca. He would have provided a wonderful future for you. I thought you'd marry him."

"We weren't right for each other, Mom."

She sighs. "Couples sometimes have bumps in the road. You need to work it out. Tell him you're sorry for whatever happened."

I tap the top of the champagne bottle. "Let's crack this open. I need a drink."

"You need to talk to Kieran," my mom insists. "Men like him don't come along very often, sweetheart."

"I sure as hell hope not," I snap. "I found him in bed with his assistant today, Mom, so it's over. Forever."

Her cheeks blush pink. "What? How could he do that to you?"

Thurston swoops in to save the day. "Karma will get him, Angie."

I almost feel sorry for my ex because in Thurston Marks's world, he sets karma in motion. If you cross the man or someone he loves, he'll come for you, and it will sting.

Chapter 7

Roman

I stand and turn when I sense her walk into Rolly's Pub.

A glance at my watch confirms what I already knew. Miss Marks is always on time.

I arrived twenty minutes ago and ordered my usual. Rolly slid it over to me with a smirk and his standard question about how I was doing.

He has no real interest in my life, only my wallet.

I told him that if he arranged to have Miss Marks's drink in front of her within a minute of her arrival, he'd be rewarded appropriately.

Since he's hastily pouring vodka into a glass, I'd say he's earned the hundred I'll tip him before I leave.

"Mr. Hawthorne," she greets me as she approaches. "It's good to see you."

The light blue wrap dress she has on showcases her lush curves. Her hair is rolling in waves over her shoulders. She takes a long, slow look at me.

Attraction is often muted in my world.

Women come into my office with the intent to work out the details of how they want their estate distributed after their death. It's hardly a breeding ground for desire.

But this place screams of anonymous meet-ups that lead to raw fucking.

Miss Marks has been calculated with her interest so far, but today something is different.

Her smile is broader and her stance more relaxed.

Maybe some lucky bastard was in her bed last night, or perhaps that look on her face is because she wants to take me home with her today.

"Miss Marks," I say her name. "Join me."

I motion toward the empty barstool next to me.

She plants her round ass down on it, squirming until she finds just the right position. A cross of her toned legs gives me an excellent view of a sliver of her inner thigh.

My teeth want a piece of that.

"It's Bianca," she finally offers her first name. "Please call me Bianca."

Something has indeed changed.

Rolly moves to deposit the glass a little to the left of her. She thanks him with a smile and a quiet word about how gracious he is to remember her favorite drink.

I stare at her profile as I take my seat.

Beauty is subjective, but there are women you meet who steal the air from the room because they are so striking.

Bianca Marks sits atop that category.

The guy sitting at the end of the bar agrees. His hand is grazing the outside of his jeans over what I assume is a pencil-thin dick, judging by the size of the rest of him.

He doesn't stand a chance with her. That doesn't stop him from keeping his eyes trained to the front of her dress.

I inch closer to her. "Tell me what's changed, Bianca."

Her perfectly arched brows dart up. "What do you mean?"

I drop my gaze to her hands. There still isn't a ring sitting on that finger. I checked as soon as she sat down next to me two weeks ago.

I wanted her then, but she was toying with me. Her amusement covered the need that was flowing from her.

She's not smiling now.

"Something is different since I last saw you." I take a sip of bourbon. "Is it the job?"

She runs the tip of her fingernail along the rim of the glass in front of her until she reaches one lime wedge. She picks it up before her tongue darts over the sour flesh of the fruit. That's followed by a nip of her teeth on it.

Her expression never changes as she sucks on it briefly.

My cock has been hard since she walked in. Now, it's aching with want.

"It's not the job," she confesses as she drops the lime onto a paper napkin sitting atop the bar.

I steal a glance at the loser who is still running his hand over his jeans as he watches her.

"It's a man then."

The fact that I don't form it as a question gets her full attention. "Why would you assume that?"

"Your phone has been buzzing non-stop since you sat down." I motion to where her purse is slung over the barstool next to her. "You strike me as the type of woman who takes her work seriously, so your avoidance of whoever is trying to reach you indicates it's an asshole."

"An ex-boyfriend," she clarifies. "He's the asshole who is texting me."

I didn't anticipate wandering down this road, but I'm game. "Why is he an ex-boyfriend?"

Her hand darts to my forearm. "I caught him in bed with his assistant last week."

"He's an idiot."

"An idiot who thinks there's a chance I still want him." Her hand slips from my jacket. "Why would I take back a man like that?"

"You wouldn't," I say even though I have no frame of reference for my assumption.

"Have you ever cheated on a woman?"

"No," I answer quickly. "If a woman I've been sleeping with isn't someone I want to continue sleeping with, I'll make that clear to her before I move on to someone I want to…"

"Sleep with," she finishes for me.

"Exactly."

She wiggles her ass on the stool. "Are you…"

"Sleeping with anyone now?" I take the question in the direction that I want to answer. "No, but I want to."

"You do?"

"With you," I say, keeping my gaze locked on her face.

Her blue eyes widen. "What?"

I lean closer to her so the over-the-pants-masturbator doesn't catch wind of our discussion. "There has been something going on between us since you walked in here two weeks ago. I feel it. You do too. You're no longer entangled with your asshole cheating boyfriend, so I'm making my intentions clear."

"Talk about not mincing words." She takes a sip of her drink. "You're jumping to a pretty big conclusion if you think I have sex with strangers."

I fight to hold back a smile. "So I'm a stranger?"

"All I know about you is your name and that you practice estate law."

"I never mentioned what type of law I practice."

Her cheeks flush. "You did."

"Liar," I accuse. "You looked me up."

"So what if I did?" She laughs it off. "I was curious."

"You still are."

She lets out a breathy sigh. "I searched for you online, Roman. That doesn't mean I'm going to jump into bed with you."

I move to stand before I slide two bills from my wallet and drop them on the bar. "I'm due in court within the hour, so we'll have to pause this discussion for now. I'll see you next week, Bianca. Same place. Same time."

I walk away because I know that I'm not imagining the energy that is bouncing between us. I made it clear what I want. The ball is in her court now. I fully expect her to volley it back to me a week from now, if not sooner.

Chapter 8

Bianca

"Did you tell Kieran to go to hell?" Maren Morgan, one of my closest friends, turns around to ask me that question.

I motion for her to take a step forward as the line we're standing in inches ahead. "More than once."

She cups a hand around her growing baby bump as she moves closer to the counter where two baristas are taking orders. "Do you think he got the message?"

He should have. Last week, after Kieran called me repeatedly, I packed up the two shirts and one pair of jeans he had left at my apartment, added a note telling him to stop contacting me, and sent it to his office. Then I immediately blocked his number.

The unopened package was returned to me the next day, so I shipped it all to his apartment.

Kieran thought it was a good idea to drop by my office to thank me with two dozen roses.

I refused the flowers with a bitter laugh.

He fell apart. He told me he lost his job the day I caught him with Ulla. It seems her boyfriend caught them in the act, too, because she butt dialed him at the beginning of their romp last Tuesday.

Her boyfriend was Kieran's boss up until that moment.

I don't know if he was looking for sympathy when he confessed that to me, but all he got was a shake of my head before I told him to go to hell.

I haven't heard from him since.

"He got it." I round her as she approaches the barista counter. "Can I get one herbal tea for the mom-to-be? I'll have a dark roast, no sugar, but add a small splash of cream, please."

Maren sighs. "I'm craving chocolate, but I shouldn't."

I scan the menu of Palla on Fifth. "Can we get one chocolate scone and a piece of banana bread?"

The barista smiles. "You bet."

I feel Maren squeeze my shoulder. "You know I like that bread for a mid-afternoon snack."

I pull out my credit card. "If you can resist it for that long."

She laughs as the barista writes my name down on both cups. I come here daily, so the fact that she knows me isn't at all surprising.

I wait for the barista to run my card before I slide it back into my wallet. I turn around to see Maren headed toward a table, so I fall in step behind her.

"I have a meeting in an hour," I warn her as we take our seats. "It's going to eat up the rest of my day."

Maren sags into the wooden chair. "I have a nap in an hour."

I let out a laugh. "Weber is kicking your ass?"

Weber is not only Maren's maiden name, but it's also the name of the baby she's expecting. She tossed around dozens of names with her husband, Keats, before settling on that for their son.

"I'll be glad once he's here." She glances at the red blouse and black pants I'm wearing. "I can't wait to get back into my normal clothes."

The outfit she's wearing is cute. The green short-sleeve top complements her red hair, and the jeans she has on are dark-washed. The low-heeled shoes on her feet have been her favorite for most of her pregnancy.

"Is it too soon to ask if you've met anyone since you dumped Kieran?"

I smile at the barista when she delivers our drinks and Maren's treats on a tray. "Thank you."

I wait until she's walking back to the counter before I answer the question. "There's a guy that's always at Rolly's pub at the same time as I am."

"Rolly is too old for you."

I laugh. "The last few times I've been in there, a man has been sitting on a barstool drinking alone."

Maren breaks off a piece of the scone and pops it into her mouth. "How many times have you seen him there?"

I wiggle three fingers in the air.

"What's he like?"

"Intense." I laugh. "Arrogant. Ridiculously hot."

"He sounds like your dream guy." She winks. "So you've talked to him?"

I nod as I take a sip of my coffee. "During our last conversation, I told him about Kieran. He had a few things to say about that."

"Keats did too." Maren sighs. "He was pissed, Bianca. He wanted to go down to Kieran's office and wring his neck."

I don't bother mentioning that Kieran is currently unemployed.

"What did the mystery guy at the bar say about Kieran?"

I hold back the detail of Roman's name because I know Maren. She'll have her phone in her hand to Google him before I finish saying his surname.

"He said that now that I was single, he wanted to fuck me."

The piece of scone in her hand falls to the table. "He didn't say that."

"He said he wasn't sleeping with anyone but wanted to sleep with me."

Her hand rubs her forehead. "What did you say to him?"

I laugh as I rest my hand on her forearm to reassure her. "I told him I don't get into bed with strangers."

She leans back. "Really good sex can cure a broken heart."

My eyes widen. "You're serious?"

"I know your heart isn't broken, but it has to hurt." She lowers her voice. "You haven't talked much about your feelings, but I know you. You're tough on the outside, but inside…"

"It did hurt," I say honestly. "It was more a bruising of my pride than anything."

"So heal it by having sex with the guy from the bar."

"I can't believe you're suggesting that." I swallow another mouthful of coffee. "You're the one who is always checking in on me when I go on a date. You've told me to be careful more times than I can count."

"That's true," she agrees with a nod of her head. "This time, I'm telling you to have fun. Don't go back to his place. Use a condom and call me with all the details when it's over."

"If it ever happens," I say. "He's gorgeous, but his assumption that I'll jump into bed with him is both hot and infuriating."

"You want him to work for it?"

I lower my voice. "I don't know. I want something. Besides, I'm not even sure I'm going back to Rolly's anytime soon."

"I can't drink anything other than water there, but if you need backup, I'm there for you." She rubs her belly. "We both are."

I smile. "I've got this. I need to run soon, so let's catch up on you. Tell me everything about the nursery."

Her face lights up. "I know it's just a nursery, but I want to give him the best life I can."

I have no doubt that she will. Her baby has parents who adore him and many people who can't wait for him to arrive.

I sip my coffee, listening to her talk about the color scheme for the nursery and the curtains she bought that have a teddy bear pattern on them.

Maren's joy is in having a family. I'm not there yet. I'm not sure I'll ever be, but I love seeing my friend living her dream.

"You have to come over and see the progress I've made." She finishes the last bite of the scone. "Does tomorrow afternoon work? Can you take a longer lunch? I'll whip up something."

Tomorrow is Tuesday.

"I'll tell my boss I'm working from home." She laughs because she married her boss.

Maren and Keats run Morgan Sports Management as a team.

"I'll make that salad you love." Her smile brightens. "The one with the avocado and bacon and that dressing that we can't get enough of."

I should say no so I can go to Rolly's and play *will-I-or-won't-I* with Roman, but my time with Maren has been limited recently because we've both been busy. I have nothing pressing on my schedule for tomorrow afternoon.

Maybe this lunch invitation from my friend is a sign. A break from men may be just what I need.

"How can I resist that?" I tap her hand. "I'll be there."

Chapter 9

Roman

"You look like you got stood up." Thomas Harrell, my business partner, and friend walks into my office.

I laugh that off, even though he hit the nail on the head. I spent two hours this afternoon at Rolly's Pub waiting in vain for Bianca Marks to show up.

"You're thinking about the Rockford case, aren't you?" He assumes the way he always does. "I told you I'd handle it, Rome."

I haven't thought twice about that case since Mr. Rockford's kids came storming into our offices looking for a piece of his estate.

The will was read right after the funeral as requested by the dearly departed.

There were a few gasps in the room, some choice curse words fired in my direction, and a declaration that the will would be fought in court.

What do you expect when someone dies with two estranged kids?

The wars that wage in courtrooms after death are almost always powered by greed. It drives people to try and get their hands on what's left behind.

Thomas skims a hand over his light brown hair. "You were supposed to meet with Clarice Blanchard this afternoon to go over her will. You blew her off."

I glance up from my desk to where he's standing a few feet away. "I rescheduled."

It was a risky move. Clarice's estate is vast. The majority of her wealth is to be directed toward a handful of charities after her death. Those change as her interests change.

She wasn't thrilled when I called her yesterday to postpone our meeting until tomorrow. I did it to clear my afternoon for Miss Marks. I didn't realize that would be a waste of my time.

"Why?"

I expected the question. Thomas thinks that we need to share everything when it comes to work. I disagree. He has his clients. I have mine. Occasionally, one of us will go to bat for the other.

"I'm not answering that."

He laughs. "I know where you were, Rome. That's not a secret since you've been going there every Tuesday for years."

"Not every Tuesday," I correct him. "I thought I'd need more time today. It turned out I didn't. End of story."

I look past him when I see my executive assistant approaching the doorway. "I'm flattered that you care enough to notice."

"Mr. Hawthorne." My assistant, Chad, taps his knuckles against the doorjamb. "I found that information you requested, sir."

Thomas's gaze volleys between Chad and me. "What information?"

I push to my feet. "That's none of your business."

"I'm getting a *fuck-off-Thomas* vibe coming from you." He laughs. "Should I close the door on my out?"

"Please." I nod. "I'll catch up with you later."

He knows that's not true. Once the clock hits six, I'm out the door. The days of work monopolizing my life are over.

"Tomorrow then." He flips his hand in the air to toss me a backhanded wave. "Later, Rome."

Chad pushes a piece of paper at me as soon as the door clicks shut. "I wrote down everything I could find."

I scan it. "You found all of this in thirty minutes?"

He shrugs. "What can I say? I'm good at my job."

I glance at the paper again. "I hate to admit it, but I'm impressed."

He huffs out a laugh. "I'm taking my girlfriend to dinner with her folks, so I'm leaving now. I need to pick up my best suit from the cleaners."

I look over the three-piece navy suit he's wearing. "I pay you enough that they should all be your best suits."

He taps a hand against the lapel of my dark gray suit jacket. "You're a Berdine kind-of-guy. I'm still shopping off the racks."

Mention of the designer brand that I typically turn to makes me laugh. "Point taken."

His gaze drops to the paper in my hand. "My search resulted in a couple of images of her. She's beautiful. Who is she?"

"You know better than to ask that."

He pushes a strand of blond hair back from his forehead. "It was worth a try."

"Go home." I gesture toward my office door. "Make a good impression on your future in-laws."

Both of his hands dart in the air. "I'm too young to be thinking about marriage, Roman."

"Does your girlfriend know that?"

I don't bother trying to remember her name because this is his third girlfriend in six months, and I can't keep track.

A nod of his head answers that question.

"I need you here thirty minutes early tomorrow for my meeting with the Hubers."

Reaching into his jacket pocket, he slides out his phone. "It's already programmed into my calendar. Do you want me to arrange for the delivery of a dozen daisies to the mysterious Miss Marks before I take off?"

I drop my gaze to the paper in my hand. "You wrote that she loves daisies. How the hell do you know that?"

He gestures to the laptop on my desk. "Look at her socials. She's always taking pictures of daisies and posting them on Instagram."

When I asked Chad to find out where Bianca works, I had no idea that he'd stalk her social media pages. I was going to set aside time for that adventure tonight.

"I'll take it from here." I point at the door. "Goodnight, Chad."

He taps the face of his watch. "It's not even four, old man. Goodnight to you too."

I huff out a laugh. "I only have five years on you."

"That's true." He pockets his phone. "But you've got a lifetime of experience behind you."

He's right. I do. I use it on a daily basis at work and in my personal life.

I plan on using some of it to convince Miss Marks that I'm worth her time.

Chapter 10

Bianca

My time spent with Maren yesterday afternoon was exactly what I needed. We ate the salad she prepared, and shared a bottle of sparkling apple juice, and then we dove into painting a stencil design on the nursery wall.

By the time Keats came home from work at eight p.m., the final touches of the nursery were complete.

Maren and her husband shared a special moment as they stood in the middle of the room and took it all in. My heart bloomed with happiness for them.

Maren hasn't had it easy the past few years, so to see the smile on her face brought me comfort.

I did stroll by Rolly's Pub on my way home even though I knew Roman wouldn't be inside. I may have missed my chance with him, but after what I went through with Kieran, a self-imposed time-out from cocky men is just what I need.

Kieran and I slept together for the first time on our second date.

I wouldn't call it a mistake, but his arrogance is what lured me to his bed.

That kind of intensity is not what I need right now.

My plate is full with work.

"Bianca!" John calls to me from where he's standing outside his office. "Can I get a minute with you?"

I dart to my feet. The bottom hem of the red skirt I'm wearing sways just above my knees. I run a fingertip over the buttons on the front of my white blouse to make sure everything is in place.

"You're about to get good news," Paige attempts to whisper from her desk. "The project in Tribeca is back on track."

My mouth drops open. "What?"

"You killed it at that meeting on Monday afternoon, Bianca." She points a finger toward John's office door. "I heard him on a call before you came in this morning. He said you lit a fire under the contractor."

I subtly threatened the man with a reminder that he still hadn't secured his place on an upcoming project we have planned in Brooklyn.

Being Thurston Marks's stepdaughter does have its perks, including learning negotiating skills from one of the best.

I set off toward John's office feeling proud of myself.

This is what happens when the stars align, and I focus on work. I accomplished something that my boss wasn't able to.

"Bianca!"

I stop mid-step when I hear another man's voice calling my name. I turn slowly because there is no way in hell that it's the man I think it is.

Except it is.

Standing near the elevator, with a bouquet of pink daisies in his hand, is the one person I didn't expect to see at my office. Ever.

Roman Hawthorne, dressed sharply in a three-piece navy blue suit, smiles at me. "Hello again, Miss Marks."

***

I stand near the top-hatted mannequin in John's office and watch as he tries to interest Roman in one of his latest projects.

I'm not surprised.

Anyone who enters John's orbit dressed in anything designer becomes a potential investor in his eyes.

I gaze down at the pink daisies in Roman's hand.

They're beautiful.

Daisies have been my favorite flowers for as long as I can remember. It's likely because they would grow wild in bunches in a park across the street from the apartment building my family lived in when I was a child.

When I glance up, Roman's gaze is pinned to me even though he's speaking to John. "It's something I'd consider after thorough research, of course. For now, I need a moment alone with Bianca."

The slight promise from Roman that he'd even consider investing in the residential tower that John has been planning in Long Island City for the past twenty years is enough to placate my boss.

"I'll see myself out." He bows to Roman before he heads toward the door of his office. "You two take as much time as you need."

"We'll be quick," I say.

"Or not," Roman adds.

I give my head a shake as John scurries out, shutting the door behind him.

I turn to Roman. "What are you doing here?"

He pushes the bouquet toward me. "I wanted to see you, Bianca, and I thought these might brighten your day."

I reach for the flowers. "Thank you, but how did you find me? I didn't tell you where I work."

"It wasn't that hard to figure out," he says, studying my face.

"It wasn't?" I cock a brow.

"It's not as though I'm a stalker. I'm a man who is curious about a beautiful woman."

"Is there a difference?" I glance down at the daisies. "You looked me up online."

"Something like that," he admits. "Just as you looked me up."

If we're keeping score, he's ahead of me by a few points. I saw where his office was located when I first searched for details about him.

The difference between us is that I didn't march down to his building and show up unannounced.

"Since you weren't able to meet me at Rolly's yesterday, I'm here to ask you to have lunch with me today at Nova."

He throws out the name of the best restaurant in the city like it's a fast food place anyone can walk into and demand whatever's on the menu.

"I'm busy," I lie.

"Dinner then."

"Busy still." I add a smile to complement my deceit.

He looks me over. His gaze lingers on my legs before it travels slowly past my breasts to my face. "Tomorrow, Bianca."

I shake my head. "That won't work."

That answer is based in truth. I'm meeting my cousin Sabrina Marks for dinner tomorrow. She's also my landlord. Sabrina owns the building I'm currently living in. We check in with each other over dinner once a month, so I can give her the insider's scoop on what's going on with her property.

Typically, that involves whatever gossip I glean from Lester. I never ask about the people who live in the same building that I do. Lester always offers, which is why I try very hard to keep him out of my personal business.

Roman's eyes narrow. "I don't give up easily, Bianca."

"I don't give in easily," I counter.

His lips curl up into a smile. "I'm a persistent man. Patient as well."

I stare at him, not sure if I'll ever get used to how ridiculously handsome he is. "The first is expected. The second is surprising."

He takes a step closer to me. "You strike me as a woman worth waiting for."

"I am."

He cocks a dark brow. "I'll be in touch soon."

"You don't have my number," I point out. "Or do you?"

With a shake of his head, he breezes past me. "That would make it too easy, wouldn't it? I'm always up for a challenge."

I hold back a laugh. "You think I'll eventually sleep with you, don't you?"

He stops and turns to look at me again. "We both know that's a rhetorical question."

"Your arrogance is…"

"Just one of my charms," he interrupts. "Goodbye, for now, Bianca."

"Goodbye," I whisper as he opens the door and walks out. "For now."

Chapter 11

Bianca

John's need to talk to me earlier was interrupted by Roman, so when the devilishly good-looking lawyer made his way out of Packton's offices, John rushed back in to see me.

He praised me for my work on getting the Tribeca project back on track, and then he surprised me with an office of my own.

It's small and cramped with a wooden desk that looks like it's been glued back together a time or two, but it's mine.

I spin around to admire my decorating skills.

Circus themes don't work for me, but soft colors and framed photographs do.

I have an image of my mom and Vivi sitting atop my desk and a picture of my dad next to it. It was taken a year before he died. His brown hair is falling into his blue eyes. His hand is raised in greeting to my mom. She's the photographer behind my most treasured possession.

That photo is the only one of him that I have framed. My mom didn't have a lot of images of my dad so I kept this one on the wall of my bedroom until today. Family pictures aren't part of the décor of my home.

My apartment is filled with artwork that Thurston gifted me with over the past few years. He's always insisted that an investment in art is the perfect birthday present.

Since his taste mirrors mine, I've never complained.

Each time he's had a painting delivered to my apartment, he's arranged to have it hung up by the building maintenance people. He's on a first name basis with all of them since his niece, Sabrina, owns the building.

It was Thurston who suggested I move into the building since the rent on the apartment was a good deal. I suspect that I'm paying less than any of the other tenants, but I like the views. It's not my forever home, but for now, it's fine.

This office feels more like mine than my apartment does, so I dashed home to get things that I know will make me smile when I'm having a rough day.

I glance at the soft pink and gray throw pillow sitting atop the window seat. I nabbed it from a chair in my bedroom. I also grabbed a silver vase from a cupboard in my kitchen. The daisies Roman brought me have found a home there.

"I love this," Paige interrupts my thoughts as she appears at the open doorway of my office. "You need to get a placard for the door that says your name."

I wave her in. "I'll work on that. I only moved in two hours ago."

She steps forward. "You didn't waste any time."

When John told me about the office, I didn't want to give him a chance to change his mind, so I ran to claim it as soon as he dropped the keys in my hand.

"Life is short," I quip. "And offices around here are rare."

She jerks a thumb over her shoulder toward where her desk sits among a sea of other desks. "You're telling me."

I move toward the corner window. "You're more than welcome to work in here when I'm out on a site."

Her eyes catch mine. "Thanks. So, I've been dying to ask you…"

I anticipate what she's about to say, so I cut her off before the question leaves her. "I met him at a bar, Paige. What do I need to do to keep you from telling Vivi about him?"

A smile tugs at her lips as she lifts her hand in the air. "I swear to keep it to myself if you tell me everything. How long have you known him? Does he have a single brother?"

Touching one of the daisy petals, I laugh. "I don't really know him. I saw him at a bar a few times. I have no clue if he has a brother."

She nods. "He's got the first step in the how-to-sweep-a-woman-off-her-feet move down pat. He showed up here looking like sex in a suit with your favorite flowers."

I tear my gaze away from the daisies. "I'm not going to be swept off my feet by anyone."

Paige's smile falls. "Don't let what happened with Kieran make you bitter. I was cheated on too once, so I know from experience how much it sucks."

I'm not surprised that Paige knows about Kieran. I expected Vivi would tell her. "I'm sorry that happened to you."

"I let it consume me." She sighs. "I should have found myself a hot suit with superb taste in flowers right after I dumped my ex."

I try to hold back a grin. "There's still time."

Heading out of my office, she huffs out a breath. "I know. That's why I'm always on the hunt."

***

"A promotion and your own office?" My cousin, Sabrina Marks, raises the glass in her hand in the air. "Let's toast to that."

I clink my water glass to hers.

We opted not to drink alcohol tonight. That has nothing to do with a deliberate decision and more to do with the fact that we're sitting in a diner that has a limited selection of beverages.

Our plan was to have dinner at Axel Tribeca, but there was a mix-up with our reservation, so we decided to head to our favorite place for burgers and fries.

Crispy Biscuit has been a staple of our relationship since we met. Sabrina is a few years older than me, so when I joined the Marks family, she already knew all the larger-than-life personalities I suddenly found myself related to.

She took me under her wing and announced that we were cousins.

That connection may have been grounded in my mom's marriage to her uncle, but we've built on it. We're friends now.

I glance at the oversized menu on the table in front of me. "I'm going all out tonight."

Sabrina's green eyes narrow. "I know what that means. You're going for a double cheeseburger and an order of fries. Gravy on the side."

I nod. "You know it."

She scratches her head behind her ear. "I should have the same, but I'm trying to behave."

"This is a celebration." I smile. "I got a promotion, and you bought another building."

Running her fingers through her brown hair, she laughs. "I decided not to follow through on the walk-up on the Upper West Side."

I'm surprised. Since Sabrina inherited a dozen properties from her father, she's been consumed with growing her portfolio. His unexpected death from a heart attack changed her life's path in more ways than one. She was in college, pursuing a degree in liberal arts when she found herself at the helm of a growing real estate investment empire.

She studied business part-time as she learned the ropes from her dad's right-hand man and Thurston. My stepfather's knowledge of real estate investing came from lengthy discussions with his older brother.

He's still mourning that loss, and I sense every time Thurston invests in a property, he secretly hopes he's making his big brother proud in some way.

I've always understood that since I've tried to do the same in my own life since my dad passed away.

"Let's celebrate your ability to recognize when a building will be nothing but a money pit."

She raises her glass again. "Cheers to that."

I laugh as she downs half of the water in one gulp. "Are you imagining that's vodka?"

Her head shakes as her gaze volleys from my face to something behind me. "I'm not. I'm also not imagining that a gorgeous man is staring at you right now."

I furrow my brow. "Define gorgeous."

"On a scale of one-to-ten, he's infinity." She laughs. "He's a stunner."

"How do you know he's not staring at you?" I question. "You're looking hot tonight in that cute black dress."

She glances down before she wags a finger at me. "What about you in that red number?"

"I thought we were eating at Axel Tribeca." I sigh. "I would have worn a wrinkled sweatshirt and jeans if I knew we were coming here."

Laughing, her eyes widen. "That guy is headed in our direction, Bianca."

As tempted as I am to turn to look at the man she's talking about, I don't. He's probably going to breeze right past us to the table near the corner where four college-aged girls are having the time of their lives as they share a giant sandwich.

I watch my cousin's expression as he approaches. The smile on her face broadens as she tucks a lock of her hair behind her ear.

"Bianca?" I hear his voice as soon as his hand brushes against my bare shoulder. "It seems we both have excellent taste in food."

I glance up, knowing who I'll find standing next to me.

Roman Hawthorne, wearing a pair of faded jeans, a gray T-shirt, and a ball cap, smiles at me.

Dammit.

Sabrina's right. Even dressed down, the man is a stunner.

Chapter 12

Bianca

I'm reasonably sure that Roman can see right down my dress. It's low-cut enough that the top of my breasts are visible from his vantage point.

I watch him fight to keep his gaze on my face, but he's losing that battle.

"I'm Bianca's cousin." Sabrina darts to her feet to present her hand to Roman.

He takes it for a shake. "It's good to meet you, Bianca's cousin."

"Sabrina," she says with a laugh. "I'm Sabrina Marks."

He glances at me before he sets his attention back on her. "Roman Hawthorne."

"Roman Hawthorne," she repeats his name. "Bianca didn't tell me anything about you, so fill me in."

I try to shoot her daggers with my eyes, but she counters with a wicked smile.

"Thirty-two, attorney, Mets fan," he says. "I'm here picking up some take-out."

Sabrina inches closer to him. "How do you two know each other?"

I push to my feet because I'm not about to let Roman lead that discussion. I don't need Sabrina to know that I was downing vodkas on Tuesday afternoons at Rolly's Pub.

Sabrina and I discovered the pub together one night six months ago. We stumbled on it after we viewed a building nearby that she was considering investing in.

"Bianca was at Packton's offices when I dropped by yesterday," Roman announces before I can come up with a lie about how we met. "John has a project that I may invest in."

I glance at him to find him smiling at me.

"I have yet to decide if it's a wise move on my part to partner with him," he adds.

I can't tell if he's serious or not. He's a lawyer, not a real estate mogul. Unless he's amassed so much wealth that he's tossing it around Manhattan the way Thurston does.

"Would you like to join us?" Sabrina motions a hand toward the small table we've been sitting at. "I can pull up a chair right next to my cousin for you."

I give my head a slight shake. "Roman said he was picking up his take-out. I'm sure he has someplace he needs to be."

"Roman!" As if on cue, Jo, the woman who owns the diner, calls out his name. "Your food is up!"

His gaze darts over his shoulder. "I'm on my way!"

"It looks like you have a big appetite." Sabrina gestures to the two large brown paper bags in Jo's hands.

Roman pats his rock-hard stomach through the thin material of the T-shirt. "I'm not easily satisfied."

Sabrina laughs. "One of Jo's cheeseburgers is enough to satisfy me."

"What does it take to satisfy you, Bianca?" Roman asks with a tilt of his chin.

I stare into his dark eyes, drawn deeper by the intensity of his gaze.

I can't tell if we're still talking about food, so I clear my throat in a desperate attempt to break the moment between us. "You should go get your order. You don't want it to get cold."

A ghost of a grin floats over his mouth. "I'll do that."

"Bianca will see you soon," Sabrina offers. "I'm sure you'll need to discuss more details about John's proposal with him in person."

Roman's gaze volleys to her before it settles back on me. "I will see you soon."

I fall back into my chair when he turns to walk away.

Sabrina does the same. "Holy hell, Bianca. Did you see how he looked at you? He'd eat you right up if you gave him a chance."

I let out a nervous laugh. "He's an intense person. He looks at everyone that way."

"Yeah, no." She shakes her head. "Mark my words, Marks. That man wants you."

I finish what's left of the tepid water in my glass. "Let's forget about him and order dinner."

Her gaze darts beyond my shoulder. "Mr. Intense is leaving. You'll keep me updated on what happens between you two, right?"

"There won't be anything to update." I run my fingertip along the edge of the menu. "I'll probably never see him again."

Sabrina laughs because she knows what I know. That's a lie.

***

Meet me at Bow Bridge in Central Park tomorrow at 6 PM.

My gaze flits from the masculine handwriting on the small piece of paper I'm holding toward the closed door of the washroom.

As soon as Sabrina was out of her chair and on her way across the diner headed for the washroom, I bolted for the counter to pay for our dinner.

Sabrina rarely lets me treat her, so I wanted to beat her to the punch tonight.

Someone already did that.

Jo slipped me the note I'm holding when she told me that Roman covered the cost of our dinner.

She seemed smitten as she told me how often he randomly pays for the dinners of people he spots in the diner when he comes in to pick up take-out.

I hear my cousin's shoes tap against the tile floor, so I shove the note in my purse.

Sabrina stops just short of the table. "You just put something in your bag. Are you going to tell me that dinner is already paid for?"

I'm not about to confess that Roman paid for our meal. Knowing Sabrina, she'll feel the need to send him a handwritten note thanking him. That would put him one degree closer to my personal life, which is precisely one degree too close.

Standing, I nod. "It's all taken care of."

She reaches for my shoulder. "I wish I could hang out longer, but I want to get a jump on a meeting I have in the morning. I need to prepare for it."

I know that feeling all too well, so I take her in for a hug. "It was great seeing you."

She tugs me closer. "I've missed you. Let's do this again soon, Bianca."

When we break apart, I smile. "Maybe next time, Axel won't mess up our reservation."

"Everything turned out the way it was supposed to tonight," she says with a hint of a smile playing on her ruby red lips. "I got to meet Mr. Intensity, and he got to see most of your tits. So it's a win-win for the two of us."

Laughing, I gaze down at my dress. "Remind me never to wear this again."

"I'm accepting hand-me-downs." She drops her hands to her hips. "I don't have as much to work with as you do, but isn't that what push-up bras are for?"

"I'll have it dry cleaned and delivered to your apartment." I gesture toward the door. "Are you ready to go?"

"I'm ready to see you happy." She tilts her head. "Give Mr. Intensity a chance. I highly doubt he'd disappoint you."

I sigh. "Sabrina…"

She winks. "If you know what I mean."

My head falls back in laughter. "I know exactly what you mean."

"Every woman should have sex at least once with a man like that."

"Why?" I ask through my ongoing laughter.

"Do it, and you'll have the answer to your question," she states. "Report back once it's over, or better yet, do it again and again before you give me all the juicy details."

I nudge her in the side with my elbow. "Weren't you in a rush to get back to your office?"

"I'm going." She takes one step toward the diner's door. "Kieran is part of your past. It's time to start moving toward your future. Promise me you'll do that."

"I'll do it," I assure her.

I will do it. The future is waiting for me, and according to the note in my purse, Roman will be waiting for me at Bow Bridge tomorrow. I just need to decide if meeting him is the right move for me.

Chapter 13

Roman

Being stood up twice in one week doesn't bode well for any man's ego. Fortunately, I'm not just any man. I'm determined. I'm also giving Miss Marks some leeway in the form of a few extra minutes before I deem this attempt at a thoughtful gesture a complete and utter fucking failure.

I glance to the left and then to the right.

The only people on Bow Bridge are an older couple holding hands and a woman pushing a baby in a stroller. She's cooing in a high-pitched voice to the infant who is oblivious to where they are.

The woman doing the cooing offers me a brisk "*hello*," as she passes me. The way her gaze rakes me from head-to-toe isn't surprising. It's a warm evening in Manhattan, and I'm dressed in a gray three-piece suit.

I smile and extend a greeting in the form of a nod of my chin.

She darts past me at a hurried pace when the baby starts crying. The cooing morphs to repeated promises that the baby will be fed soon and everything will be all right.

I trail her with my gaze until I spot heaven in heels on the approach.

Jesus.

Bianca Marks is, without question, one of the most beautiful women on this planet.

Her hair is blowing in the breeze, her body is wrapped in a dark green shift dress, and nude heels with impressive height are on her feet.

She has her nose buried in her phone as she takes one quick step after another. Her gaze only darts up to check the path in front of her.

We finally make eye contact when she's ten feet away from me.

I hold back a grin. I sense she's doing the same.

The fact that she showed up, albeit fifteen minutes late, is enough to plant a broad smile on my face for days.

"Roman," she says my name in a breathless rush.

A mental image immediately forms of her whispering that in my ear when I'm inside of her.

We'll get there. I have no doubt.

For now, I'm savoring the chase.

"I had a meeting that ran late," she explains. "But I'm here now."

Her gaze drops to my hand and the single daisy I'm holding.

"For you," I say, handing it to her.

"Thank you." She takes it with a smile before she glances around at the landscape of blooming trees and freshly cut grass. The lake is calm tonight, as is the breeze. "Why am I here?"

Running a finger over my chin, I bite back a laugh. "I'm not reason enough?"

Her eyes dart to mine. The color of them is mesmerizing. It's darker than sky blue but lighter than a sapphire. "I haven't decided yet."

I can't say I've ever experienced anything similar to the game we're playing. I like it. It's fuel for the undeniable desire I feel every fucking time I'm within a foot of her.

I step closer to her by half a step. "Do you recall that I mentioned that I hoped that we'd have a chance to celebrate your promotion in my favorite way?"

Her gaze drops to the front of the dress she's wearing. "Yes."

I follow her lead. Her body may be hidden from view, but the material of the dress hints at what's underneath. I've imagined for days what she would look like in my bed.

I'm not surprised by her assumption that when the stars align and I have reason to celebrate, I do it with my dick.

I wouldn't pass up the opportunity to do that with her. Hope springs eternal that's on the near horizon, but tonight, the celebration is more deeply rooted in tradition than raw carnal need.

"Every time I've accomplished something memorable, I come here." I wave my arm in a wide arc. "I've been doing that for a very long time."

"Here?" She questions with a tap of her shoe against the bridge deck.

I nod. "I come to this spot and indulge in one of my favorite things."

Her eyes widen. "What?"

She watches with rapt focus as I tug a gold foil-wrapped bar from the inner pocket of my suit jacket. "Chocolate."

A sigh of relief escapes her. "Oh, candy. You like candy?"

"Chocolate," I correct her gently. "I bought a chocolate bar with my very first paycheck when I was twelve. I rode my bike here and ate the entire thing."

Her gaze drops to the bar in my hand. "You have excellent taste. Wolf Candy makes the best caramel chocolate bars in the city."

"It's much better than the first one I bought when I was a kid." I tug on a corner to reveal the chocolate. "You'll share it with me?"

She nods. "I won't pass that up."

I break off a piece and hand it to her, even though I want to slip it between her lips.

She takes it and nibbles on a corner. Her eyes close for a second. "Chocolate after a long day at work is never a bad thing."

I pop a piece in my mouth, allowing the milk chocolate to melt on my tongue.

She keeps her gaze trained on my lips the entire time.

"I might have to take up this tradition as a way of celebrating my major life accomplishments." She smiles. "When I was twelve, my way of celebrating didn't involve chocolate."

I'll take any insight I can get into the mysterious Miss Marks. "How did you celebrate when you were twelve?"

"Pinball."

Holding back a grin is impossible, so I don't even attempt it. "Pinball?"

"We moved into a new apartment building around that time. It had a game room. The pinball machine was my favorite." She smiles. "I loved playing that thing, so whenever I brought home a great report card, my mom would give me ten dollars. I'd trade it in for quarters at the bodega around the corner from our building and then play pinball for hours."

"Hours?" My brow perks. "You must be a fucking wizard at pinball."

"I am," she states proudly as she reaches to grab another piece of chocolate. "I'd beat you."

"Prove it," I challenge.

That lures a hearty laugh from her. "How? I haven't been inside that building in years."

"I know where we can find a pinball machine," I tell her.

She eyes me skeptically as she sucks chocolate from the pad of her thumb. "Are you going to say it's at your place?"

I bite the corner of my bottom lip to ward off a smile. "I assure you I don't need to resort to that to get a woman into bed."

Her gaze locks on mine. "I didn't say that."

"You implied it."

She laughs. "Where's the pinball machine, Roman?"

"Easton Pub," I say. "We can grab a drink. Play some pinball."

She studies my face. "I'm not sure."

I gaze down at the daisy in her hand. "Let the flower decide."

Her brow twists in confusion. "What?"

I reach forward to pluck off a petal. "Pinball it is." I pluck another. "Pinball it isn't."

"That doesn't seem like a wise way to decide how I'll spend my evening."

I pluck another and let it fall to the deck of the bridge. "Pinball it is."

She takes over, plucking each petal, muttering to herself as she does.

Just as she reaches the last one, she raises her voice. "Pinball it is."

"Lucky me."

"No," she sighs, shaking her head. "Lucky me. I told you I'm good, Roman."

I lean forward, bending enough that my lips are near her cheek. "I have no doubt about that, Bianca."

She takes a step back. "This isn't a date."

Smiling, I nod. "Noted."

"This is a celebration."

"Understood." I inch back to take her in. "It's a celebration, not a date. I'm clear on that."

"Good," she says, straightening her shoulders.

"My driver is waiting for me." I step to the side to allow her to take the lead. "Easton Pub awaits."

"I need to be home by eight."

As do I, but I don't offer that. "Is that your curfew?"

Shaking her head, she purses her lips. "Are you always this not-funny?"

"Always."

Laughing, she sets off ahead of me. I follow behind, completely infatuated with this woman.

Chapter 14

Bianca

The drive from Central Park to Easton Pub might have been filled with non-stop flirting if I hadn't received a panicked call from a contractor.

Since I took on my new position, I no longer have the ability to redirect calls like that to the senior project manager. That's my role now, so I spent my time sitting next to Roman in an SUV, reassuring the contractor that I'd be on-site first thing tomorrow morning.

As soon as the driver parked next to the curb on the street in front of the pub, Roman was out of the car. He rounded it quickly to open the car door and extend a hand to help me out.

Chivalry may be a lost art, but Roman has it down to a science.

I stand to the side as he tries to beat my high score on the pinball machine that I darted to as soon as we were inside the pub.

Roman handled the drink order at the bar. He brought me a glass of vodka and cranberry juice. It was just the way I like it with two lime wedges on the rim. He opted for what looks like sparkling water.

I'd feel guilty about drinking alcohol when he's not, but I need the liquid courage.

Sitting next to him during the ride here was intoxicating. He smells wickedly good, and his gaze never left me.

That hasn't changed since we've been in the pub.

At least three drop-dead women have walked past us, but Roman has kept his attention solely on me until it was his turn to play.

He pushes the flipper buttons rapidly, trying to keep the ball in motion.

"You're losing," I point out with a tap of my fingernail on the top of the machine.

"I'm aware," he says with a straight face. "You weren't kidding when you said you're good, Bianca."

I smile. "I'm better than good."

His eyes catch mine for the briefest of moments. "Tell me something else about you."

I take the last swallow of the drink in my hand. "Twenty-seven, senior project manager, New York Yankees fan."

His fingers stop as he turns to face me. "You're joking."

I watch the small white ball slip out of play and out of view. "I won."

"You distracted me," he points out. "With a lie about being a fan of that other New York baseball team."

I laugh. "That other team? So you don't even say their name?"

He shakes his head. "Never."

"It seems we've come to an impasse." I sigh. "I'm a lifelong New Yorker who knows which ball team is the best."

His gaze sprints over my face. "I'm a lifelong New Yorker with a few years on you, so suffice it to say, I have more knowledge when it comes to which team is superior."

"Is that how you argue in court?" I ask with a grin. "It's weak."

"Weak?" A smile ghosts his mouth. "I'm anything but weak, Bianca."

I don't need him to tell me that. He wears strength like one of his well-tailored suits. Everything about him screams masculinity. Power is etched in the nuances of his deep voice and how he moves. He commands attention.

I drop my gaze to the glass in my hand. "Do you want a rematch?"

"So you can distract me again?" He takes the glass from me. Bringing it to his lips, he tilts it until one ice cube slides into his mouth. "I should have ordered a bourbon."

I watch the way his tongue darts out to collect the last lingering drop of my drink from his bottom lip. "There's still time."

He glances at his watch. "Unfortunately, there's not. Your curfew is creeping up on us."

I reach for his wrist and twist it so I can see. "You're right."

His hand moves to hold mine. "Did you enjoy your celebration, Bianca?"

I don't fight his grasp. Instead, I relish it. The warmth of his hand sends goose bumps scattering up my arm. "Yes."

"What was the best part?"

"Beating you," I say quickly. "The chocolate was a close second."

His free hand dives into the inner pocket of his suit jacket. He tugs out another chocolate bar. "For your next craving."

I drop his hand to take it. "You didn't buy an extra for yourself?"

His eyes look into mine. "No. I bought that one just for you."

"You assumed I'd like chocolate as much as you do."

He lowers his voice. "I assume you like many things as much as I do."

With effortless ease, he shifts the conversation from chocolate to sex while still holding my gaze.

I look away. "Thank you, Roman."

"I can have the driver take you home," he offers. "I promise to keep my eyes closed so I won't know where that is."

I can't fight a smile. "I'll get home on my own."

I wait for him to ask for another non-date, but he just stares at me.

"Thank you for the chocolate and the drink," I say. "And thank you for sucking at pinball. My winning streak still stands."

He huffs out a deep laugh. "A rematch is in our future."

I'm tempted to ask when, but I don't.

"I'll walk you out." He motions toward the door of the pub.

Disappointment nips at me. He's not even trying to move in for a goodnight kiss.

I fish my phone from my purse. "I'll order an Uber. I think I'll wait in here until it arrives."

A smile slides over his mouth before he leans down to press his lips against my cheek for a soft kiss. "Congratulations again on the promotion, Bianca."

My whispered "*thank you*" gets lost when he turns to walk away, leaving me wondering when I'll see him again.

Chapter 15

Bianca

I prepare to devour the chocolate bar that Roman handed me as soon as I enter my apartment. Unfortunately, before I can tear it open, it falls from my hand.

"You scared the hell out of me," I accuse with a pointed finger in the air.

Holding a large white bowl in her hands, my sister half-shrugs. "I ran out of microwave popcorn."

"That's what stores are for." I sigh. "You could have said something as I was walking in, Vivi. My heart is beating like crazy."

"Take a few deep breaths," she says soothingly. "Do you want some popcorn to go along with your chocolate?"

"I want my keys back." I laugh.

"You don't." She plops herself on my couch. "When you gave me those keys, you said I could drop by whenever I wanted and make myself at home. So I'm doing that."

It's another I-told-you-so moment with my dear little sis.

Vivi stretches out her bare legs. She's wearing a pair of jean cut-offs and a white off-the-shoulder sweater she stole from my closet more than a year ago. It suits her better than it does me.

She's always been effortlessly beautiful. Vivi can wake up and look flawless without a stitch of makeup.

"How was work today?" she asks.

Picking up the chocolate bar, I smile. "Good. I'm really enjoying my new position."

She pats the empty spot on the couch next to her. "Come and sit with me."

I settle in beside her with the chocolate bar still in my hands. "How was your day?"

"I met with three engaged couples." She smiles. "They all want to get married in late summer, but we're booked up through the rest of the year."

"You'll squeeze them in."

Her eyes light up. "I will. How can I get in the way of someone's fairytale happy ending?"

My sister has always been a romantic deep into her bones. She'd hold elaborate weddings for her dolls when she was a kid and wrote love letters to her future husband when she was fourteen.

"If you're willing to share the chocolate, I'd be forever grateful."

I run a fingernail over the label to break the seal. Carefully peeling back the foil wrapper, I stop when I notice something peeking out from beneath the chocolate. "Why don't I get us something to drink? Is lemonade good for you?"

"Perfect," Vivi says before she drops a piece of popcorn into her mouth.

I trek across the apartment with the chocolate bar tightly in my grasp.

Once I reach the kitchen, I place it down on the counter and edge the wrapper off the bar. I tug on the corner of what looks like a white piece of paper.

When it's completely free, I flip it over.

An uncontrollable smile blooms on my lips as I read what's written in the same masculine handwriting that was on the note Roman left me at the diner.

Meet me on Saturday at noon. Crispy Biscuit.

I'll be the guy holding the daisy.

I glance down at the package again.

The seal matches the seal of every other Wolf Candy chocolate bar I've ever eaten.

How the hell did he sneak that note inside of it?

Roman Hawthorne is full of surprises.

"Is everything okay?" Vivi asks from where she's sitting.

I scoop the note into my hand, folding it in half, and then again before I slide it into a kitchen drawer. "Everything is great."

She pushes to her feet. "I'll come help with the lemonade. Have you eaten yet? I can order something in for us."

With my heart hammering inside of my chest in anticipation of seeing Roman again, I smile. "You choose."

"Me?" She laughs. "What's gotten into you? You always control our take-out choices."

"It's your turn to choose."

She eyes me skeptically. "You seem extra happy tonight. Either your new job is agreeing with you, or you met someone. Which is it?"

I drop my gaze. "It's the chocolate."

She lets out a laugh. "It is good, but I know something better. Nova has this salmon dish with olives and artichokes. Are you game to try it?"

"Let's do it," I say as I round her to head to my bedroom. "I'm going to jump in the shower before dinner."

"Sounds good," she calls after me. "Hey, Bianca?"

I turn when I hear the softness in her voice. "Yes?"

"I like seeing you this happy." She smiles. "It makes my heart sing."

Leave it to Vivi to bring tears to my eyes. "I love you, V."

"I love you, B," she says softly. "A little bit more than yesterday."

Chapter 16

Roman

I spot Bianca before she can get her eyes on me.

She's chatting up Jo, the owner of Crispy Biscuit. From where I'm sitting, their discussion is light-hearted and fun. Bianca's hips are swaying back and forth as she shuffles from one heeled black boot to the other.

I'm getting my fill of her curvy ass in a pair of faded jeans. She's topped that with a blue short-sleeve sweater. Her long hair is gathered into a ponytail that's sitting atop her head.

I glance down at the jeans and T-shirt I'm wearing.

"Roman!"

I look up when I hear my name called. I recognize the voice immediately as Jo's.

"Your lunch date has arrived," she says as she approaches me with Bianca on her heel.

Bianca's head shakes slightly. "It's not a real date."

Jo's gaze darts over her shoulder. "Call it what you will, but you two are endgame."

Bianca stops suddenly in place. "Endgame?"

"I'm right about this." Jo laughs as I push to stand. "I know a perfect match when I see one, and I'm looking at perfection now."

Bianca's eyes are pinned on me, but I'm not diving into that conversation. My life is too full to even think about anything beyond dating. I've had a handful of casual relationships the past few years. They've satisfied the needs I've had at the time.

"I'm looking at perfection," I add to try and steer this onto a different course. "You look great, Bianca."

Her reaction to how I'm dressed is exactly what I expected.

She laughs. "Did you wear that shirt on purpose?"

I smooth my hands over the New York Mets logo on the front of my T-shirt. "What do you think?"

"I think you should take it off."

My hands drop to the bottom hem. I tug it up far enough to give her and Jo a clear view of the abs I work hard for. "Will do."

"Wait." Bianca's hand reaches to stop mine. "I didn't mean right now."

I know she didn't, but the tease was worth it to see her reaction. "Later, then?"

"Let's have lunch." She settles on a wooden chair across the table from where I was seated.

Jo drops one menu in the middle of the table. "Give me a shout when you're ready to order."

I take my seat again. "How long did it take you to find my note?"

The corners of her full, pink lips edge up. "Not long. How did you get it inside the wrapper?"

"Magic?"

She shakes her head. "Try again."

"I know the owner of Wolf Candy," I admit. "Nikita Wolf. I asked if she could do me a favor. She obliged."

"She's a friend?"

I can sense that she's fishing for more, so I give it to her. "Nikita has been my sister's best friend since pre-school. I consider Nikita my sister too."

"Does that come with perks?" Her eyebrows draw up. "Do you get free candy?"

I do, but I'm not about to admit that I have a sweet tooth that is never satisfied. "Sometimes."

"Lucky," she quips.

"Very," I counter. "I'm having lunch with the most beautiful woman in this city."

She holds my gaze. "You're charming as fuck, but you know that, don't you?"

Fuck.

The word conjures up a mental image of her beneath me as I take her in long, slow strokes.

I shake it off with a chuckle. "Charming as fuck?"

"You know it." She taps her palm on the table.

"I know that I'll never lie to you," I say with confidence. "I'm about to have a meal with the most striking woman I've ever seen."

Her eyes lock on mine. "You're nice to look at too."

I tug on the front of my T-shirt. "Even dressed like this?"

She nods. "I'm pretending that doesn't exist."

A chuckle escapes me as I slide the single daisy I brought across the table. "This exists."

She scoops the stem into her palm before lifting it to her nose to inhale its scent. "Thank you. Will I need it to help me make a decision today?"

I adjust my ass in the chair so I can lean forward. "What decision might that be?"

I want to hear her say that the need to get naked with me is just as strong for her as it is for me.

"Whether I should have a BLT or a cheeseburger."

I reach to cover her hand with mine. "Save the flower. I'll order both, and we can share."

Her gaze drops to our hands. She doesn't move to pull away, so I scoop her hand into mine.

"I'm glad you came, Bianca."

She lifts her chin to look at me. She takes a second to study my face. "Me too."

I take that as a positive sign. She showed up. She's smiling, and the day is young.

I stand by what I said. At this moment in time, I'm the luckiest man in this city.

Chapter 17

Bianca

I hold tightly to the stem of the daisy as I walk out of Crispy Biscuit with Roman on my heel. I tried to pay for our lunch, but he insisted on covering it.

It was chivalrous and welcomed.

Kieran and I split the cost of one too many meals down the middle at his urging.

"Thank you again for lunch, Roman."

"It was my pleasure," he says as he holds the door to the diner open for two women rushing inside.

They both stop to admire his smile.

The taller, blonder one moves a step closer to him. "What do you recommend for lunch?"

He defers to me with a raised brow, so I answer. "The cheeseburger is the best."

Both of the women laugh in unison. The blonde pipes up again. "No burgers for us. We live on salads."

"I'm sorry to hear that," I offer with a straight face.

A hearty chuckle escapes Roman.

The women say something to each other before they disappear into the diner.

Roman lets the door handle slip from his grasp as it closes behind them. "I couldn't survive on salads alone either."

"I like food," I admit. "I really like good food."

He falls in step beside me as we make our way down the crowded sidewalk. "What else do you really like?"

"Daisies." I wave the flower in the air. "Did you figure that out when you were stalking my socials?"

He glances at me. "You post a hell of a lot of pictures of daisies."

I bring the flower to my nose to take another whiff. "Each one is a little different, so I try and capture that."

He smiles. "That makes sense."

"What do you really like?" I ask.

He scoots around an approaching couple holding hands. "You."

I half-expected that to be his answer. "You don't know me."

"I know that I like you," he admits. "My stance on how I feel about you hasn't changed, Bianca."

We round the corner headed nowhere in particular. "You're talking about what you said at Rolly's Pub, aren't you?"

He nods. "I want to take you to bed."

I take a quick look at the people around us, but everyone is so focused on where they're going that they don't notice us. "You believe that's where we're headed?"

"Now?" He laughs. "If you're down for that, I'm ready, willing, and able."

I stop to face him. "You want to have sex with me now? As in right now?"

He pivots, so he's looking right at me. "Let me make it crystal clear. I want to fuck you. I've wanted that since we met."

Heat pools between my legs as my common sense battles with desire. I step closer to him to lower my voice. "Are you always this direct with women?"

"I'm always honest."

I can't complain about that, so I don't. "Is that our endgame, Roman? We go somewhere, fuck each other, and part ways?"

He leans so close to me that I can feel his breath skirt over the skin of my neck. "You're making me unbearably hard, Bianca."

My gaze darts to the front of his jeans and the obvious bulge. "Roman."

"I want you," he says in a whisper. "The ache is real, but no, I'm not going to fuck you and walk away."

I take a measured step back to catch my breath.

"I like hanging out with you," he goes on. "I want more of that too."

I try to piece that together in my mind. "What are you saying?"

"I want to date you, Bianca." He reaches to touch my forearm. "I want to take you to bed. I want both."

Panic drives the next words out of my mouth. "I just got out of a relationship."

He nods. "I'm not looking for anything serious."

I lock eyes with him. "What are you looking for?"

"Fun. I need fun. I sense you do too, so let's have it together."

"Just fun?" I question to be clear. "Nothing serious? I just got this promotion and with the break-up I need for things to be..."

"Uncomplicated?" he interrupts. "You have my word that I'm not looking to put a ring on your finger."

I laugh. "Thank God."

He joins in with a chuckle. "I'll always be straight with you. When this stops working for either of us, we tell the other. No bullshit games or hidden agendas. We're two people with undeniable chemistry so let's act on it."

I gaze down at the flower. "You make it sound so easy."

"It is easy, Bianca."

I take a step back. "Is it?"

"Yes," he affirms with a slight nod of his chin. "I like my life just the way it is. Work is a beast, but I do it because I love it. I sense you're dealing with the same thing with your promotion. Our connection is the escape we both need right now."

I laugh. "This is the strangest conversation about sex I've ever had."

With a hand on my forearm, he backs me up until I'm resting against the brick exterior of a building. "You're not used to discussing sex before you have it?"

I shake my head. "I'm used to things being more organic. There's the first look followed by some flirting. A really great first kiss, and then we get to the first..."

"Fuck," he finishes my sentence. "We've had that first look. We've flirted, so what's next? The kiss?"

"Here? Now?" I shake my head. "I like spontaneity, but we're in the middle of a crowded sidewalk on a Saturday afternoon."

"Is this not the time or place for one of those really great first kisses?" A smile ghosts his mouth.

I stare at his lips. "I didn't say that."

"The when or where of an amazing kiss matters a hell of a lot less than the who part of that equation," he points out.

I can't disagree, so I nod.

He rests one hand on the brick behind me. His body towers over mine as I look up at him. "You want to kiss me right now, don't you, Bianca?"

I almost laugh at the question because it's the only thing I've wanted to do all day.

He knows the answer. I see it in the way he's looking at my lips. He expects me to reach up and plant one on him now.

"The flower holds the answer to that question." I raise it and brush it against his chin.

With a furrowed brow, he glances down. "The flower?"

I pluck one petal from the daisy. "Kiss him now." I pluck another. "Kiss him never."

He huffs out a stuttered laugh. "Never? Make it later, Bianca. We both know our first kiss is on the horizon. It's just a matter of when it'll happen."

If arrogance were currency, he would be the richest man on the planet.

I pluck another petal. "Kiss him now." I lock eyes with him as another petal falls from the flower. "Kiss him never."

He fights a smile.

I pluck my way around the daisy, keeping my eyes trained on his.

He finally breaks our gaze as my fingers grab the delicate last petal.

"Kiss him never," he whispers.

I pluck it off and let it float to the ground. "Kiss him never."

His tongue darts out to coat his bottom lip. "Fuck the flower, Bianca."

As much as I want to lean forward and press my lips to his, I don't. I won't. Instead, I rest my back against the wall. "I'd say best two out of three, but I only had the one flower."

His gaze darts to the right and then the left. "Stay right here. Don't move."

I hold in a laugh as he takes off in a sprint to the left toward a fresh flower stand that's half a block away.

Chapter 18

Roman

I grab hold of two bouquets of daisies. I'm determined to kiss Bianca today. If that means she needs to pluck her way through dozens of flower petals this afternoon, I'm all in.

Until four o'clock. Once the clock strikes that hour, I need to end this date.

I consider it a date.

I have no fucking clue how Bianca is viewing this mid-day meet-up.

Stealing a glance in her direction, I catch her staring at me.

I wave the flowers in the air before I motion at the vendor who is busy talking to a man who can't seem to decide between a large bouquet of red roses or a smaller arrangement of pinks ones.

Impatience drives the next words out of my mouth. "Buy her both."

He turns to me, and I immediately notice that I'm face-to-face with a college-aged kid. He can't be more than eighteen or nineteen years old. "I wish. I can't afford both."

I shove a hand in my back pocket to retrieve my wallet. I pull out a hundred-dollar bill and hand it to the vendor. "This should cover all the roses in his hand and the daisies in mine."

The gray-haired woman smiles as she takes the money. "Let me get your change."

"No need," I tell her.

She thanks me with a smile before she moves toward a woman holding a lavish bouquet of what looks like wildflowers.

"I can give my girlfriend all of these flowers?" The guy standing in front of me asks. "Did you seriously just buy them so I can give them to her?"

"You bet."

"I need your number so I can get in touch." He tries to hold both bouquets in one hand while he fishes in his pocket. "I've got my phone. Give me a minute to find it."

I shake my head. "Consider it a gift."

He huffs out a nervous laugh. "No one has ever done anything like this for me before. Are you sure you don't want me to pay you back? I get paid a week from Wednesday."

"Buy your girlfriend another bouquet then," I suggest.

"Will do." He smiles. "I'm going to do a good deed for a stranger today too. I'll pay it forward."

"There's a plan," I say quickly. "I need to run. I've got a beautiful woman waiting on me."

He glances over my shoulder. "I think I spot her. She hasn't taken her eyes off of you since you walked over here."

That's music to my ears.

I spin around to find Bianca on the approach. A smile lights up her face.

"Thanks again, man." The kid with the roses pats my shoulder. "You just made my day."

Mine was made the moment Bianca showed up at Crispy Biscuit. It's only going to get better from here on out.

***

Bianca's gaze volleys from the daisies in my hand to the back of the kid with the roses as he takes off in a sprint down the sidewalk.

"What just happened?"

I glance down at the flowers. "I bought you daisies so I can score a first kiss before this day is over."

She brushes her fingers against my bicep. "Did you pay for that guy's flowers, Roman? From where I was standing, it looked like you paid for those roses he was holding."

"I did."

"Do you know him?"

"No," I answer honestly. "I know that he wanted to put a smile on the face of a woman who is special to him, so I helped him out."

Her blue eyes search my face. "Do you do stuff like that often?"

"Stuff like what?" I ask, knowing full well what she means.

"Buy something for a stranger?"

Someone once told me that the key to a good man is his willingness to do what's right for others. I try to live by that.

With a hand on her lower back, I guide her away from the flower stand. "He was short on cash."

She walks beside me slowly, contemplating what I just said. "Most people wouldn't do that for someone they've never met."

"I try not to concern myself with what most people would do." I smile. "I do what works for me. He needed a hand, so I offered what I could."

Her steps slow as we near the spot we were standing at when she plucked the daisy's petals off. "The world needs more people who feel that way."

I turn to face her. "You can get to work pulling these flowers apart, Bianca. I'm hoping luck will be on my side, and I'll get that first kiss we were talking about."

Her gaze drops to the daisies before she looks into my eyes. "Luck is on your side."

I take a step closer to her because if that's true, I'm about to get a taste of her lips. "Is that so?"

"Yes." She perches on her tiptoes and grabs a fistful of my T-shirt to tug me even closer to her.

I don't say a word.

I scoop my hand around her waist, pull her body against mine and press my lips to hers for what I hope to hell is just the first kiss in a million more to come.

Chapter 19

Bianca

His lips are as soft as I've imagined they'd be. I fall into the kiss, letting myself feel everything that has been building inside of me since the first time I saw Roman's face.

My hand finds the back of his neck as the kiss deepens.

I lose all sense of time and place. The sounds of a busy weekend day in Manhattan quiet as everything stills inside of me.

When the kiss finally breaks, he looks into my eyes.

Before he can say anything, I whisper his name. "Roman."

He kisses me again, but this time it's soft and gentle. His hand moves to my chin. He cups it in his fingers as he steps back. "That was one hell of a first kiss."

I smile. "You're telling me."

His gaze drops to the daises that are still in his hand. "I'm glad I didn't have to leave that to fate."

I am too. His kiss was everything I'd hoped it would be and more.

I've never felt this on fire from just a kiss before.

We stare at each other. No words pass between us, but what does is a feeling that's impossible to describe. I'd call it anticipation, but that's too tame for it. The desire is strong, but it's buried beneath something more intense. It's a need that I've never felt for a man before.

"Mr. Hawthorne?"

We both turn at the sound of a woman's voice. The smile on her face is genuine. The kindness in her eyes is unmistakable.

"Mrs. Blanchard," Roman says with surprise in his tone. "How are you?"

"Happy to see that you have a life outside the office." Her hand moves toward me. "I'm Clarice Blanchard, and you are…"

Her voice trails as she waits for me to introduce myself, so I do as I take her hand for a soft shake. "Bianca Marks."

"Bianca Marks," she repeats my name. "It's nice to meet you."

"You too," I offer.

Her gaze shifts from my face to the daisies in Roman's hand. "Those are beautiful. I'm obviously interrupting a special moment."

I'm the first to shake my head. "You're not. I was just about to take off."

I don't add that I need space so I can catch my breath. That kiss was more than I expected, and the reaction my body had to it is still lingering. I feel a sudden need for fresh air even though I'm standing under the sun with a warm breeze rushing over me.

"You're Thurston's daughter, aren't you?" Tilting her head, Clarice steps closer. "He's talked about his brilliant Bianca. That's you."

Even though I'm tempted to explain to this woman that my connection to Thurston is based on my mom's marriage to him, I don't. Instead, I nod. "Yes."

She grins. "He's very proud of you."

I smile in response because I don't know what to say. I'm grateful for Thurston's support. I've told him as much.

"I'll have to tell him I met you." She looks to Roman. "You're a lucky man, Mr. Hawthorne. From what I've heard from her father, Bianca is an incredible woman."

I didn't expect a stranger to sing my praises, but who am I to argue with her?

"Indeed she is," Roman says with his gaze pinned to me. "If you'll excuse us, I'm going to say goodbye to Bianca."

Clarice takes the hint with a measure of grace. "Of course. I'll stop by your office on Monday. I have another small adjustment I want to make to my will."

"I look forward to seeing you then." He turns to look at her. "Enjoy the rest of your day."

"You too." She glances at me. "It was a pleasure to meet you, Bianca."

I can honestly say the same, so I do. "I'm glad we had the chance to meet."

With that, she turns and walks away, leaving me feeling as though I got a small glimpse into Roman Hawthorne, the lawyer.

I liked what I saw.

***

"Thank you again for lunch and the flowers."

Roman pushes both bouquets at me. "You're sure you don't want me to help you carry these home? I can arrange them in a vase next to your bed."

I do want that, but not yet.

I'm still processing how that kiss made me feel. I need time before I get into bed with him.

I gather the flowers into my arms. "I think I'll be fine on my own."

He nods. "I'd move in for another kiss, but all eyes are on us at the moment."

He's right. A pretty brown-haired woman with six children is standing behind him. All the kids have their gazes pinned on Roman.

A small girl elbows the boy next to her. "It's him."

I suspect she meant to whisper that, but she can't be more than four or five years old. Whispering takes practice. I know some adults who don't have that skill mastered yet.

"Leave him alone," the boy says. "He's with that pretty lady right now."

Roman's brows perk. "The pretty lady he's referring to has to be you."

The smile on his face lures one to mine.

He jerks a thumb over his shoulder toward the children. "Let me guess. Three girls, two boys, and a redheaded toddler."

I glance around him to get a better look. "You're good at this."

"The smallest girl is doing all the talking," he says. "Or she's about to."

As if on cue, the little brown-haired girl approaches Roman and taps his palm. "Hey, Romeo. It's you, right?"

Romeo.

I fight to hold back a laugh.

The woman holding the toddler clucks her tongue as she approaches the small girl. "Let Roman be, sweetheart. It's impolite to interrupt."

"I'm not interr…interpupting," she stutters. "I'm saying hi to him. He said we should when we see him."

"Excuse me for just a minute," Roman says to me.

I nod because I can't wait to see what's about to happen.

He spins on his heel. "It's all good, Mika."

The woman holding the toddler breathes a heavy sigh of relief. "They spotted you from the corner. They wanted to say hello."

The five kids all join in on a chorus of hellos before the little boy Mika's holding whispers, "hi," in the softest, sweetest voice.

The oldest boy waves to me. "Hey, lady."

"Hey," I attempt to wave back with a hand that is buried beneath the bouquets.

"This is Mika." Roman steps to the side to give me access to the mom. "Mika, meet Bianca."

I shrug and laugh because I can't reach out to greet her.

She chuckles. "Those are beautiful flowers."

"So pretty," one of the girls says. "They're daisies."

"They are," I affirm with a nod of my head.

"We love daisies," she whispers. "Mommy got some once. She let us each have one."

I look down at their worn sneakers and the mismatched clothes they're wearing. The youngest reminds me of Vivi with her big blue eyes and braided hair.

Roman glances back at me. "Daisies are Bianca's favorite flowers."

"Mine too," the youngest girl exclaims. "When I grow up, I'm going to paint a daisy on my bedroom wall."

"I've thought about doing that," I joke. "Roman got me extra daisies today. Do you think you could all share them?"

I balance both bouquets in my arm so I can reach around to grab the bottom of one.

"You don't have to do that," Mika whispers before she looks at Roman. "You've already done so much for us."

I look at his face to get his reaction, but his expression gives nothing away.

"I gave you a job," he says. "One that you're great at."

She adjusts the toddler in her arms. "One I wasn't qualified for."

He shakes his head. "You learned fast. Besides, one day you'll make partner with our firm. When that happens, I expect you to side with me when Thomas tells me I'm wrong about something I'm right about."

That pulls a laugh from her. "Deal."

Chapter 20

Roman

Who the fuck knew that a stroll down one city block in the middle of Manhattan on a Saturday afternoon could expose so much of my life to Bianca?

She's met a client and one of the junior assistants from my firm.

It's not as though I'm a well-known guy in New York. I work hard, I do what I can for the people around me, and I treasure my time at home.

Today, I savored the moments I had alone with Bianca, even though they were sparse.

"I have to get going," Bianca announces to everyone gathered on the sidewalk around us. She clears her throat. "That came out louder than I anticipated."

I huff out a laugh. "I got the message loud and clear."

She looks to where Mika is rounding a corner with her crew in tow. "I'm sorry I gave away some of the flowers, but…"

"But nothing," I interrupt, stepping closer to her. "I'm glad you did that. It made their day."

Her eyes search my face. "Those kids are fond of you."

There's an unasked question in those words and her expression, so I answer it. "Mika faced a hard time after her husband died. I helped out."

Her mouth falls open. "She's young."

"Thirty-nine."

Her gaze drops to the ground. "That has to be rough."

"Brutal," I agree.

"You prepared their wills? Is that how you met?"

I see no reason to lie to her, so I don't. "I met them when her husband, Brian, was in the hospital."

Concern knits her brow. "Were you a patient too?"

"No," I reassure her with a shake of my head. "Brian was on the same ward as someone I was visiting. We struck up a conversation when he was doing laps in the corridor and I passed him."

"So you stepped up to help?"

"I did what I could," I nod. "Mika had dreams of becoming a lawyer before she had kids. She's slowly working toward that, so I gave her a job to help out in the meantime."

"You did more than that." She tilts her head. "Those kids were looking at you like you're a superhero."

"I played Santa and dropped off a few gifts at their place last Christmas. Thomas, my business partner, was the elf."

A smile lights up her face. "Is there photographic evidence of this, counselor?"

"There sure as hell better not be."

She glances to her right as a trio of people breeze past us. "You surprised me today."

I know that she's talking about what she's learned about me from her brief time with Clarice and Mika, but I take the conversation in another direction. "It's the kiss, isn't it? You're going to tell me you're surprised that I'm the best you've ever had."

Her teeth land on the corner of her bottom lip in a failed attempt to halt a smile. "You think that was the best kiss I've ever had?"

"I know it was," I say confidently.

It was the best kiss I've ever had, and I saw the look on her face as soon as we broke apart. That said it all.

"It was in my top three."

Shaking my head, I reach forward to run the pad of my thumb over her bottom lip. "You're a shitty liar, Bianca."

She nips at my thumb. "You're arrogant."

I step closer. "I know that kiss sits at number one for you."

"How would you know that?" She eyes me.

I lean down to brush my lips softly against hers. "Because it's the second best kiss I've ever had."

Her gaze locks on mine. "Second best?"

I tug her closer to me again, not caring that the flowers are pressed between us. "This is the best kiss I've ever had."

I take her mouth again. This time the kiss is demanding and filled with raw need. It lures the softest sound from her.

When our lips part, she lets out the faintest moan. "Holy hell, Roman."

"The best, " I whisper as I nip at her bottom lip. "Is yet to come, Bianca."

Her lips move as if she's about to say something, but not a word escapes her. Instead, she backs away slowly. "I'm going to go."

Since I'm in desperate need of a cold shower, I don't fight her. "I'll see you soon."

"You will?"

I hold back a smile. "Yes."

I wait for her to ask when, but she leaves me with a trail of her fingers over my chin. "Thanks for everything."

I snag her hand in mine so I can plant one last kiss on her palm. "I should be the one thanking you for today, Bianca."

I stand in place as she walks away, waiting for her to glance back.

As she's about to round the corner, she finally looks my way.

The smile she gifts me with is enough, for now.

When she disappears out of sight, I take off in the opposite direction, knowing that this sudden aching need I feel inside is all because of her.

Chapter 21

Bianca

I glance at the screen of my phone to check the time.

It's nearing five. For a Monday, the hours have flown by. That's because John tossed me a curveball as soon as I arrived at the office this morning. He needed me on-site at one of our projects all day.

I took off as soon as he told me, grateful that I'd chosen to wear black pants and a gray sweater today. The overcast skies that I woke up to are to blame for that.

Running a hand through my matted hair, I sigh.

Wearing a hardhat on a job site is par for the course. If I had known that I'd be sporting one for eight hours, I never would have taken the time to curl my hair this morning.

Once I get home tonight, my plan is to shower, make a sandwich, and fall asleep all within an hour.

Footsteps outside of my office draw my attention to the open doorway.

I smile as soon as I see Paige with a grin on her face. I motion for her to come closer to my desk. "I'd get up, but I'm tired."

She lets out a giggle. "Don't take this the wrong way, but you look exhausted."

"I'm avoiding mirrors at all costs until I get home," I confess. "You, on the other hand, look adorable."

It's the black and white polka dot dress she's wearing. Her style is always on point.

"I have something for you," she says, producing a small white envelope from behind her back. "This was dropped off at reception earlier. I told Mona I'd see that you got it since she had to leave early."

Paige handles reception if Mona is out for the day or if she sneaks away early. Yoga is her life, so whenever her favorite instructor is hosting a hot yoga class, Mona is nowhere to be seen.

I take the envelope from her. My name is the only thing written across the front of it.

For a split second, I hoped it was a message from Roman, but the handwriting is feminine. I don't recognize it.

I glance at Paige. "Did Mona mention who dropped it off?"

She shakes her head. "Are you going to open it?"

I tap the envelope against my palm. "Later. I have a half dozen calls I need to get to before I leave for the day."

Her gaze volleys between the envelope and my face. I know she's as curious about what's inside as I am. "I'll guess I'll go back to my desk."

Motioning toward my office door, I toss her a sugary sweet smile. "Can you close the door on your way out? I don't want to be interrupted during my calls."

"Will do," she says with a smile. "If I don't see you before I head home, have a great one."

"You too," I call after her.

As soon as the door clicks shut, I rip open the envelope to find a white card.

My eyes scan the note that appears to be written by the same person who jotted my name down on the envelope.

You are cordially invited to the soft launch of Lise.

Tonight at 8.

I flip the card over to see an address in Greenwich Village.

I open the browser on my laptop and type Lise and the address into the search engine. The results are varied, but not one is a clue to the invitation.

I delete Lise and call up a search for the address.

It traces back to a hair salon that closed down months ago.

I know too many people in this city to ignore this. The owner of whatever *Lise* is might be the family member of an investor or the close friend of one of the contractors I've worked with.

Connections are crucial in my world.

Even though I'm tempted to invite Vivi to tag along, I won't. Knowing my sister, we'd attend this soft launch and then end up hanging out until the wee hours of the morning.

If I'm going to Greenwich Village, I want to do it on my terms.

I'll show up, solve the riddle of why I was invited, and then go home.

With luck on my side, I'll still make it to bed before the clock strikes midnight.

Chapter 22

Bianca

Choosing an outfit for tonight was easy. I went with the staple that has never let me down. It's a little black dress with an empire waist and pearl beading around the collar.

It's another gift from my mom. I gave up asking her to stop buying me things when she broke down in tears one afternoon. I had called her to explain that while I appreciated all the lavish gifts, it wasn't necessary.

I made that call while I was holding an expensive diamond-encrusted watch in my hand. She had it delivered to my apartment on a Saturday. My birthday wasn't around the corner, and the holidays were months away.

It was another one of her '*just because*' presents. Over time, I've come to understand that the gifts are her way of expressing her love. I'd much rather have the frequent tight hugs she used to give or the kisses on the forehead, but those are a thing of the distant past now.

I slipped my feet into a pair of black heels and finished the outfit off with a simple gold bracelet and earrings.

I ran a brush through my hair after I had a quick shower, so it's holding the natural wave that I loathed when I was a kid. I don't mind it nearly as much now.

Since his phone distracted the Uber driver, I asked him to drop me a block away from my destination after he took a wrong turn. It would have taken longer for him to circle back around than for me to walk to Lise.

Holding tightly to the mysterious invitation, I round the block on my approach to the address.

People mill about outside what looks like a bodega, and once I'm past them, I have a clear view of the place I'm headed to.

There's no sign on the front suggesting that the place is called *Lise*.

The awning that hangs over the door is green and white striped with a torn corner. Dark curtains shield the space from the sidewalk, so I can't peek inside. I try the door handle, but it's locked.

I turn the invitation in my hand over again to double-check the address, but I'm in the right spot.

This was either sent from the future, or someone is playing a prank on me.

"Dammit," I whisper to myself.

I could have been at home in a pair of sweatpants and a tank top stuffing my face with a sandwich washed down with a soda.

Just as I'm about to turn and walk away, the door flies open.

A pretty brown-haired woman wearing a dark T-shirt, faded jeans, and a navy blue apron smiles at me. "You must be Bianca."

I nod. "That's me."

Smoothing her hand over her ponytail, she sighs. "I'm Annalise. Annalise Brookings. Welcome to what will soon be Lise."

With a wide arc of her hand in the air, she gestures for me to walk through the doorway.

I do.

What greets me is entirely unexpected.

It looks like a bistro with exposed brick lining the walls. Assorted plants are hanging from above. The lighting is elegant, and the floors are polished concrete. I spot a kitchen near the back of the space. The smells emanating from it are incredible.

"This is beautiful," I whisper.

"Do you really think so?" she asks, her blue eyes searching my face. "I want it to be inviting but not pretentious. It needs to feel like an escape from the frenzy of Manhattan."

As the door shuts behind me, the city's noises are muted.

I turn toward her. "It's exactly like that."

"Good." She rubs her hands together. "I've prepared a little bite of everything that will be on the menu. I hope you're hungry."

I glance around. "I'm starving. Where is everyone else?"

A light laugh bubbles out of her. "He didn't tell you, did he?"

"I'm lost." I let out a nervous chuckle. "All I know is that I received an invitation to come here, so I showed up."

Her hand leaps to my shoulder. "I'm so happy that you did. Rome will be too."

Rome.

Is she talking about Roman?

I open my mouth to ask the question but slam it shut immediately when I see someone move in the kitchen. I only catch his profile, but I'd recognize him anywhere.

Roman turns just in time to catch the smile that's sliding over my lips.

I wave a hand in the air. "Hey!"

"Bianca," he calls my name out with the slightest growl in his tone. "I'm so glad you made it."

I am too.

Chapter 23

Roman

"Cousins?" Bianca's brows perk. "You're cousins?"

I swear I hear the faintest hint of relief in her tone.

Annalise nods. "We're business partners now too. I've always wanted to open my own restaurant."

The first I heard about it was when the guy Annalise was supposed to marry broke it off right before the wedding. It was a wake-up call for her. Not only did she realize that Myles, her ex-fiancé, wasn't right for her, but she also reevaluated her career choice.

Until that time, Annalise had buried her dreams of being a professional chef beneath her success as a model. She's graced the covers of magazines worldwide and appeared in the runway shows of some of the biggest names in fashion.

All of that changed when she hit restart on her life. She enrolled in culinary school, went to work in the kitchen of Nova as a sous chef, and crafted out a plan for her own bistro.

I wanted to invest. Annalise has rare skills in the kitchen. She intuitively knows how to create food that is not only delicious but a feast for the eyes. I expect some bumps in the road, but Lise has a shot at finding a spot in New York's crowded culinary market.

Bianca's gaze travels the intimate space. "I think you've got something special here, and judging by what I'm smelling, the food is going to taste as good as this place looks."

Annalise motions toward the single table that's set for dinner. "Feel free to take a seat."

She opted for a yellow rose centerpiece that's set in a short round vase. The dinnerware is white with silver trim around the edge of the plates. The glassware is simple but elegant.

I never saw myself becoming a silent partner in an eatery, but I'm glad I opted in. I'm proud of this place and happy that I could play a small part in helping my cousin turn her passion into a career.

I motion for Bianca to lead the way. She does just that as her ass sways beneath the dress she's wearing.

She's stunning. The fact that she didn't know what she was walking into speaks of her curiosity and willingness to dive headfirst into an adventure.

We've got that in common. I've embarked on my share of adventures in the past that I went into without a clue where I was headed.

All of those worked out well for me.

I hope to hell tonight does too.

***

"When do you officially open?" Bianca questions Annalise. "I'm going to tell everyone I know to come here."

Annalise's face brightens with a wide smile. "Seriously? You'd do that?"

"I need to." Bianca laughs. "Anyone who doesn't experience the food here is missing out. I can't describe how good everything tastes."

"Try," I bite out.

Her gaze darts to me. "Superb? Phenomenal? Out of this world?"

"Sublime?" I offer.

Annalise cups her hands to her chest. "You're both being too kind."

Bianca points at the empty plate in front of her. "I ate every last bite. It was all that good."

We were served sample portions of at least a dozen dishes that Annalise plans on offering. She'll circulate them out every few weeks to keep patron interest high, but anything that's in demand will earn a permanent spot on the menu.

She's explained all of this to me time and time again. I've listened closely, but at the end of the day, I signed off on giving her control of the day-to-day operations. I may have bankrolled part of this endeavor, but Annalise is the captain of this ship.

"When we have the actual soft launch, you'll come?" Annalise asks Bianca. "It won't be for another month, but I'm putting the guest list together now. Can I add you?"

Bianca looks at me.

I can sense what she's thinking. *Where will we be in a month?*

If I have my way, we'll be in bed as soon as that soft launch is over. I want the same tonight, but I have no idea what Bianca wants.

"I'll be here," she says while keeping her gaze trained on my face. "If I can help at all, I hope you'll let me know."

Annalise chuckles. "I just may take you up on that. I'll get your number from Rome."

A soft smile glides over Bianca's lips. She doesn't drop a hint that I'm still walking around town without her number in my contact list.

So far, I've seen it as more of a challenge than a burden, but that's not the case anymore.

"Are you both ready for dessert?"

Bianca sighs. "I shouldn't, but who am I kidding? Dessert is a good day's reward, right?"

Annalise pats me on the shoulder. "Rome lives by those words."

I laugh because damn right I do. They were first said to me years ago, and since then, I've said them a time or two myself.

I pat Annalise's hand. "Bring it on."

She leans down to plant a kiss on my cheek. "Thank you for everything, and by the way, I like her."

"I like her too," I say while I stare across the table into Bianca's eyes.

Chapter 24

Bianca

We stroll down the sidewalk next to each other. This evening has been perfect. The food was divine, the ambiance was warm, and Roman was a gentleman.

While we were sharing a few small dessert plates, he held my gaze for a beat too long when Annalise came over to ask how everything was.

After that, she excused herself and hid in the kitchen until Roman pushed back from the table to stand.

I thanked Annalise with a hug and a promise that I'd be back for the official soft launch. She called tonight a super soft launch. I call it a night to remember, and it's not over yet.

"You had a good time," Roman says as we round a corner.

I'm letting him lead the way. If he takes me back to his place, I know I'll need a minute to decide if that's what I want.

I can't deny that I've been thinking non-stop about what it would be like to have sex with him, but I can't say for sure if I'm ready for that to happen tonight or not.

"That didn't sound like a question," I joke.

He turns to look at me. "It wasn't asking if you have a good time. I was pointing it out."

His arrogance is becoming less annoying and more charming.

"How could I not?" I sigh. "Your cousin is a gifted chef."

"She is," he agrees with a nod of his head. "I'm glad she decided to do this. I'm not an expert, but Lise has promise."

"I think so too," I chime in as the wind picks up. "I know I'll be going there regularly."

He moves a step closer to me as a group of people strolls past us. "With me, I hope."

I'm hoping for that too.

Feeling more and more like I want him to take me home, I test the waters. "Are we headed for a nightcap?"

He stops and reaches for my hand. I stop too when I feel the warmth of his touch.

We stare at each other for a moment. Nothing passes between us but a keen understanding that this feels comfortable, important, and special in a way that, at least, for me, I've never felt before.

He drags my hand up until it's resting against his lips. "I can't tonight."

I'm disappointed and surprised, but I don't show it. Instead, I smile. "Maybe another night."

He kisses my palm before he wraps his hand around mine to hold them both against the center of his chest. "Definitely another night."

I look past him to the nearest subway stop. "I think I'll hop on the subway and head home."

His gaze stays trained on my face. "I live nearby, so I'll walk."

That stings. The fact that he lives near here but hasn't tried to take me home hits me in a way it shouldn't. Instinctively, I know it's because I'm still feeling some lingering pain over what happened with Kieran.

His infidelity was fueled by something within him, but I can't ignore the fact that there was a bite of rejection that came with it.

"Bianca," he whispers my name as he cradles my hand close to his chest. "I want you. Jesus, do I want you."

I smile.

"That text message I got right before we left Lise changed my plans," he admits. "I wish to hell I could blow it off, but I can't."

I hear the regret in his tone. I saw it on his face too when he checked his phone as we were leaving the bistro. "As long as it's not your wife or your girlfriend, I understand."

The smile on his face fades. "That's not who I am. I told you at Rolly's that I only fuck one woman at a time."

Technically, we're not fucking. I should point that out.

"I'm single." He waves his left hand in the air. "No girlfriend. No current lovers. Never married."

I didn't think I needed to hear it spelled out in such simple terms, but it's reassuring. "Good."

"I want to see you again soon."

I want the same, so I tell him. "I'd like that."

"I was going to ask for your number, but…"

"But," I interrupt. "This has been way too much fun."

"It has," he agrees with a nod of his chin. "You're eventually going to give it to me, though, right?"

"My number?"

He rakes me from head-to-toe. "Yes."

"After our next date."

"So tomorrow then?" he asks.

"Maybe." I tilt my head. "We'll have to see what the day brings."

He inches forward, his hand still clinging tightly to mine. "Kiss me goodbye, Bianca."

I press up on my tiptoes and glide my hand over his jaw. The soft stubble tickles my palm. "Goodnight, Roman."

He takes my mouth in a deep, slow kiss that stops time. I hold back a moan, desperate to feel more but scared to let myself fall too far, too fast.

I break the kiss and look into his eyes.

"You're going to kill me with need before I get my hands on you," he whispers.

I laugh and swat him across his chest. "I thought you needed to go."

"I do." He kisses me softly before he gives me one last long lingering look. "Get home safely."

I nod, turn on my heel, and walk away, hoping that tomorrow brings with it another chance for me to see him.

Chapter 25

Roman

Up until this point, I've eagerly taken the lead to secure time with Bianca. I've put in the effort, not giving a shit about what I'll get out of it. I want to fuck her, but that's not all I want.

Putting a smile on her face has become its own reward. I saw her expression when she walked into Lise last night.

She was curious, but more than that, she was excited. Her gaze darted around, and I know without a doubt that she was looking for one thing, or more specifically, one person. Me.

Her lips curved into a smile as soon as I greeted her from the kitchen.

We sat through dinner staring at each other.

It makes sense that I couldn't tear my gaze away from her, but she was just as captivated as I was.

I intended to reach out to her today to secure time with her tonight, but she beat me to the punch.

It's just past noon. I'm in my office, holding a white box in my hands. It's wrapped in a bold red ribbon. An envelope is tucked beneath it, and my name is written across the front in black ink. The handwriting is graceful, elegant, and unmistakably feminine.

It has to be Bianca's.

"This was delivered just now?" I question Chad.

"Yup," he accompanies the word with a brisk nod of his head.

"By who?"

"I didn't catch his name." He shrugs a shoulder. "He's been in before delivering documents. I'm pretty sure the gift isn't from him. He was just doing his job."

I hold back a laugh. "You can leave."

"And miss the unwrapping?" He sits down in one of the leather chairs that face my desk. "Not a chance."

"Get your ass out of here."

He sees the expression on my face. I'm trying to be stoic, but I'm about to crack a smile. "At least tell me if it's from the beauty who likes daisies."

"I won't know that until I open it in private." I point a finger toward my office door. "Shut that on your way out."

"Or you'll fire me?" He crosses his legs.

I drop the box on my desk. "Out, Chad."

"We need to talk about the Murphys." He taps the face of his watch. "Mrs. Murphy wants to come in at four instead of two tomorrow. If you can make that happen, Mr. Murphy won't have to book any time off. His shift got shifted."

I raise a brow at his corny pun.

"See what I did there?" He rolls a hand in the air. "His shift got shifted. Good, right?"

"Wrong." I finally smile at him. "Make that change now."

He tugs his phone out of his jacket pocket. "I'm on it, boss."

"At your desk."

"You can just say go to hell next time." Drawing to his feet, he laughs. "I'm ordering lunch soon, so don't text me what you want."

"Turkey on rye," I call out as he exits my office. "And a coffee."

He tosses me a wave before he shuts the door.

I reach for the envelope and tear it open. I laugh aloud when I read what's written on the card inside.

Pinball Tournament.
You Versus Me.
Friday Night at Easton Pub.

Friday? Fuck, that's three days away. I was hoping to see Bianca tonight, or at the latest, tomorrow.

Sighing, I drop into my chair before I pull on the red ribbon wrapped around the box.

I open the lid and stare at what's inside.

"What the hell?" I chuckle. "You've got to be kidding me."

Nestled in white tissue paper is a navy blue T-shirt. Front and center is the logo of a baseball team.

The New York Yankees.

Laughing, I pick it up. I spot a card under it.

I read it with an uncontrollable smile on my face the entire time.

If I win our tournament, you have to wear this for an entire day.

Your choice on what I wear if you win.

(There's zero chance in hell that will happen.)

Bianca xx

I need to practice my pinball skills because I have no intention of losing. I'm going to win, and when I do, I don't want Bianca in a Mets T-shirt. I want her nude in bed next to me.

Chapter 26

Bianca

Roman beat me to Easton Pub.

I didn't specify a time on the note I sent him earlier this week. I had hoped to be out of the office early so I would have time to stop at home, change clothes and get myself together before meeting him.

That didn't happen.

I had a five o'clock meeting that ran long. As soon as it was over, I left the office, hopped on the subway, and made my way here.

I intended to wear jeans and a cute black blouse I picked up this week, but I'm stuck in the soft gray dress I wore to work this morning.

I smooth my hands over the skirt as I swing open the door to the pub.

Roman was standing near the bar when I first spotted him through the window. His gaze was stuck on his phone, so it gave me a chance to check him out.

I'm not the only one doing that.

A blonde woman sitting next to him is staring at him.

I can't blame her. He looks amazing dressed in a pair of gray pants and a black sweater.

I watch as she taps him on the forearm. That's enough to draw his attention to her. They exchange words, and with a shake of his head, she slides off the barstool and walks away.

His gaze doesn't follow her. Instead, it shifts to the doorway. He smiles the instant he sees me.

I walk toward him, trying not to shake in my shoes.

Even though I had reservations, I took the initiative to arrange our date tonight. I'm the one who bought the New York Yankees T-shirt, wrapped it up, and had it delivered to him.

My stomach was twisting in nervous knots until a bouquet of daisies arrived at my office on Tuesday afternoon.

The note attached to them was short and sweet.

Friday, it is.
Roman

The daisies were a constant reminder that tonight we'll have another date, likely another kiss, and maybe more.

"You look stunning, Bianca," Roman says as soon as I'm near him.

I want to tell him he does as well, but the words are stuck in my throat. He's sporting late-day stubble that makes him look slightly untamed. It's a look I could get used to.

"Thank you for the daisies," I whisper as he goes in for a soft kiss on my cheek.

"I'd thank you for the T-shirt, but..."

"But," I interrupt. "I hope you have it on under that sweater. I intend on winning tonight. I expect you to start wearing the shirt at midnight."

He tugs on the collar of his sweater. "No T-shirt."

I toss him an over-exaggerated frown. "Does that mean you think you'll win?"

"I know I will," he says with confidence.

I stare into the deep brown richness of his eyes. "Arrogance is not a substitute for skill, Roman."

"I'm aware." He fights to hold back a smile. "When I'm playing for high stakes, I tend to come out on top."

There's so much hidden innuendo in that statement that I take a step back. "Roman."

"Bianca." My name rolls off his tongue with a bite in it.

I arch a brow. "You really don't want to wear that T-shirt I sent you."

He leans closer, skirting his lips over the soft flesh of my cheek. "I really want to win because I get to choose what you wear."

I almost sigh aloud when he kisses me softly and swiftly. "You're not winning. I won't be wearing a New York Jets T-shirt tomorrow."

He lifts a hand to trail his index finger over my chin. "When I win, and I will, you'll be wearing nothing tonight."

My heart pounds inside my chest. "Nothing? Tonight?"

His eyes rake me over. "You're about to lose in the best possible way. Let's get started."

I glance over at the pinball machine. What happens tonight depends on whether I can pull off a win.

Or an intentional loss.

***

"Best two out of three, Roman?" I challenge. "I was distracted, so your win doesn't count."

I'm not lying.

John decided to call me for an update about my late-day meeting as I was in the middle of a great run on the machine.

I ignored his first two calls, but panic set in, so I turned away just long enough to check my phone's screen.

It was too long.

The ball got away from me.

I took the call and spoke to my boss, while Roman blew my high score away.

I can't say I was disappointed.

The entire time I was playing, I seriously considered whether or not to throw the game to him.

Fate took the decision and ran with it.

"No," Roman says with a smirk. "I won fair and square."

"You didn't," I playfully argue. "I thought the call was an emergency, so I looked away."

He leans a hip against the machine as he listens. "We're even. You distracted me last time by bringing up the ball team you like."

"Love," I stress. "I'm a huge New York Yankees fan."

I say it loud enough that a few people near us raise their hands to pump the air and join in with chants about the team.

Roman waves them off with a wave of his hand. "The Mets rule."

"Yay, Mets!" A woman calls from the corner before a man repeats her words louder with a toast to the team.

I burst out in laughter.

"I won, Bianca." He studies my face. "You know it, and I know it, so let's stop wasting time."

"Roman," I say his name with a tremor in my voice. "Are you asking me to go home with you?"

"Or you can take me home with you." He reaches for my hand. "If that's too much, we can take this to a neutral place."

"A neutral place?"

"I'll show you." He squeezes my hand. "Are you game?"

I place my trust in his hands, and nod. "I'm game."

Chapter 27

Roman

"You don't live here?" Bianca's gaze stays trained on the view out the windows of this penthouse apartment. "Why not?"

The answer to that is too long, complicated, and personal for me to answer right now.

"It didn't feel like home," I sum everything up in that tidy package. "It's on the market, but I doubt like hell the broker will bring anyone through at this time of night."

She lets out a giggle that shakes her shoulders. "If you're selling this place, where do you live? It would have to be a castle to beat this apartment."

It's home. I live in a place that finally feels like home.

This penthouse is a reminder of a life I'd rather forget.

"It's different," I admit.

"Different as in more square feet and a better view?" She glances over her shoulder at me. "Because that's hard to imagine."

"Where do you live?"

That turns her right around. The light streaming into this main room from the hallway casts a shadow on her, highlighting her curves.

I want my hands on her now.

I need to touch her, kiss her, and feel myself inside of her.

"Madison Avenue," she says quietly. "In a building with a nosy doorman and a neighbor who thinks I steal her food."

"Sounds like the makings of a great sitcom."

She laughs that off. "I like it. My apartment is big enough for me. The rent is reasonable. I feel safe there."

"Do you feel safe here?"

I debated bringing her here, but the building is always bustling with people. We rode the elevator up with six others before they departed on lower floors. There's nothing in here that speaks of my life. I removed all the pictures from the walls, and cleared out my belongings on the day I got the keys to the three-bedroom apartment I live in now.

Sometimes, walking into the inner sanctum of another person's life can douse the heat of the moment.

It's happened to me.

I've gone home with women who wanted to give me hints into their private lives. When I'm only looking for a fuck, I don't want to see family photographs or gain insight into their decorating choices.

I want that with Bianca, but there was hesitation in her eyes when we talked about where to go tonight. I could tell that she's not ready to take me home with her yet.

"I do feel safe," she says. "I don't think you're an ax murderer."

I huff out a laugh. "I'm far from it."

She steps closer to me. "What are you?"

I want to tell her. Jesus, do I want to confess that to her. I'm more than an attorney who works hard for every dollar he earns.

"A man who wants you."

The corners of her lips curve up. "You have condoms."

"Several," I admit, tapping the back pocket of my pants.

"And high hopes." She laughs.

"Need," I say without a hint of amusement in my tone. "I have a desperate need for you, Bianca."

She inches closer still. "Need is a strong word."

"It's not strong enough to describe what I'm feeling." I keep my gaze trained on her face to see her reaction. "Want doesn't suffice either. There is a constant ache when I'm near you."

"An ache?" she questions in a whisper. "What do you mean?"

I take the last step to close the distance between us.

She doesn't hesitate when I reach for her hand and place her palm against my chest. "Feel that?"

Her eyes dart from my chest to my face. "Your heart beating?"

I nod. "It only beats like that when I'm around you. Hell, in Easton Pub, I could have passed out when I first saw you."

The smile on her lips travels to her eyes. "You liked what you saw?"

I press her hand harder against my chest as my heart hammers inside. "There's your answer."

"You make me feel special," she confesses. "Very special. I've never felt that from a man before."

She should always feel special, wanted, valued and respected.

"You're an incredible person," I say honestly. "I consider myself damn lucky that I met you."

Her bottom lip quivers. "I'm glad I'm here with you tonight."

"Me too." I reach my hands up to cup her cheeks before I take her mouth in a kiss that's only a promise of what this night will bring.

Chapter 28

Bianca

Holding Roman's hand, I follow him into the bedroom.

I can tell it's the main bedroom because of the attached walk-in closet and what looks like a luxurious attached bathroom.

There's a king-sized bed with navy blue bedding and a painting on the wall over the wooden headboard. The rest of the space is a blank canvas.

It's hard to imagine he once lived here since the open closet door gives me a view into a row of empty hangers and a shoe rack with nothing on it.

"You didn't take your bed with you when you moved?"

The corners of his lips lift. "I bought a new one. My sister lived here for a few years after I left. She moved out a couple of months ago, so I listed it. The broker staged it. This bed and another in the guest room are the only pieces that once belonged to me."

Nerves tumble in my stomach as I watch him tug on the bottom hem of his sweater.

"I'm going to slip out of my clothes," he says, watching me intently. "I'd like to undress you myself if that's all right with you."

I nod in response, my hands twisting in front of me. "I'd like that."

His answer is a swift pull of his sweater over his head to reveal chiseled abs and a rock hard chest.

My gaze follows his hands as he undoes his belt, unbuttons his pants, and pushes them to the floor.

He steps out of them along with his shoes and socks.

When he finally looks at me, he's wearing nothing but black boxer briefs.

Needing a moment to catch my breath, I point at his pants. "The condoms."

"Right." The word comes out quietly before he digs his hand in a pocket of his pants to pull out a few foil packets. He tosses them onto a nightstand next to the bed.

His head turns slowly until our eyes meet. "Tell me what you're feeling right now."

Trying to describe the rush of emotions hitting me is impossible, so I manage a small smile and one curt word. "Fine."

"Fine?" he repeats back. "You feel fine?"

Nodding, I watch as he takes slow, steady steps toward me. My gaze drops to the front of his boxers. "I'm fine."

Once he's standing directly in front of me, his hands reach for mine. "I want more than that. Are you nervous? Excited? Ready to run out of here?"

I look into his eyes. "Yes, yes, and no."

He smiles. "Good, good, and great."

I don't flinch when his hands move to the front of my dress. He holds the sash in one hand, yanking on it gently. "I'm nervous too. I'm fucking excited, and I'm tempted to lock you in here and keep you here for a week, maybe two."

I let out a bubble of laughter. "What would we do for all that time?"

His hands move deftly to undo the sash, so the dress falls open.

"Goddammit. Look at you."

I glance down at the black bra and panties I'm wearing. I had a red lace bra, and matching panty picked out to wear tonight, but since I never got home, it's still sitting in a drawer in my bedroom.

His hands glide over my shoulders to push the dress from my body. "If I had you all to myself for a week or two, I'd fuck you two or three, maybe four times a day. We'd talk about life. We'd eat good food. We'd enjoy ourselves."

His hands move again, this time to my back. He skims his fingertips over my skin until he reaches my bra.

I don't move when he unclasps it with ease or when he slides it from my body to toss it on the bed.

"I've never seen anything as beautiful as you." His voice is rough and filled with desire.

I take his hand again so I can step out of my heels.

Just as I'm about to tell him he's an incredibly gorgeous man, he drops his hands to my waist and spins us both around. I let him edge me back until my legs hit the side of the bed.

"Tell me you don't have a curfew tonight," he says as he guides me to sit on the soft blanket covering the bed.

I answer as he lowers himself to his knees. "No curfew."

His fingers move softly over my thighs, separating them with the slightest pressure. "Good. I'm going to try my fucking best to take my time, but there's no guarantee, Bianca."

I reach for his chin to bring his gaze back to mine. "Roman?"

He searches my face for something. Maybe a clue to how I'm feeling or affirmation that this is exactly what I want. I give that to him with my words and touch. "I'm yours for the night."

"And more nights?" he questions. "This isn't a one time thing."

I love that it's a statement. There's no doubt in what he's saying.

"This isn't a one time thing," I repeat.

With that, he lowers his lips to my knee and plants kisses up my thigh until his tongue brushes over my cleft through my panties.

I moan from the anticipation, and when he pushes the fabric aside for his first taste of me, I fall back against the bed, close my eyes, and lose myself in the moment.

***

His hands slide over my legs.

I groan. "Roman, please."

"Please," he repeats back in a voice strained with need. "I want this."

I wanted what he gave me; two, or maybe it was three orgasms. He ate me again and again, never letting me catch my breath.

He told me to trust him before he lapped at me with his tongue.

His moans drove me closer to the edge each time until he backed off and teased me with his fingers.

With my limbs aching as much as my pussy, he moves me gently until I'm on my stomach.

When I feel him get off the bed, I rest a cheek against the soft blanket. My eyelids crack open to see him sheathing his cock in a condom.

His eyes catch mine. "I need to feel you. If it's too much, tell me to stop."

Those words won't leave me. It's not too much. It will never be too much with him.

This man has made me feel more in an hour than I've felt with any of my former lovers during those relationships.

I feel cherished and desired.

He moves around me. When I feel him crawl onto the bed, I try to roll over, but he stalls my movements with his hands on the back of my thighs. "Like this, Bianca. You'll feel me so deep inside of you."

I know I will.

Nodding, I moan when I feel the first brush of the head of his thick cock against my cleft.

He lets out a guttural sound when he inches close to my opening, and that first push inside pulls a moan from us both.

As he straddles my thighs, holding my hips in his hands, he plunges his cock into me, again and again.

I claw at the bedding, wanting more and more.

"Fuck," he grits out. "So good."

"So good," I repeat under my breath because it is. Not just the sex but him. He's everything, this is everything, and as I climax, I call out his name.

That's enough to drive him wild.

He fucks me intensely, with each thrust deeper than the last until he comes with a shuddering groan.

Chapter 29

Roman

I fucked her from behind because I'm a goddamn coward.

I knew that if I looked into her eyes when I was buried inside of her, that I'd be lost to her forever.

Tonight was too much for me.

It wasn't just the fuck. It wasn't the way her body felt or how she tasted. It was all of it. The gentle sounds she made when I kissed her, the way she pleaded with me as I ate her out.

It's how she's looking at me now.

She's on her back on the bed staring at me. We've been this way for the past ten minutes. Silence is sitting between us, but it's not awkward.

It's reassuring, comforting even.

I've never wanted to be this close to a woman after sex. Yet, with Bianca, I want to stay here all night.

"I should go home," she whispers.

"Not yet."

A smile blooms on her swollen lips. I kissed her senseless after we fucked. I rolled her over, crawled over her, and pressed my lips to hers.

The kiss was just as sensual as the fuck.

It was intimate. It made me feel vulnerable in a way I haven't before. I felt centered, full, satisfied.

"Why not?" she questions.

I grin when her index finger runs over my bottom lip. "I want more."

A gentle nod of her head confirms she wants the same as I do.

Her hand glides from my lips to my chin before it drops to my chest. "What we did was incredible, Roman."

She drops her gaze to my semi-hard cock.

I reach for her hand and guide it to my dick, circling her fingers around it. I guide the pace of her strokes. "I promise we'll do more incredible things."

Her lips part as I harden even more under her touch. "I know we will."

My eyes close as she ups the pace of her strokes. The pad of her thumb inches out to circle the head of my cock with each pass of her hand over it.

"Roman," she says my name in barely more than a whisper. "Tell me something I don't know about you."

I open my eyes to the sight of her beautiful face mere inches from mine.

I drop a hand to her stomach to trail my fingers over the soft flesh until I part her folds. I glide my finger over her clit. "I like you."

She circles her hips. "I thought that you might."

I try to huff out a laugh, but a deep-seated groan falls from me when she squeezes my aching dick.

"You like me a lot," she says.

I nod. "Guilty."

Her lips find mine for a soft kiss. "Fuck me, again. I want to see your face when you fuck me."

At this moment in time, I'd give her anything she asked of me.

After circling her clit again and then again with my fingertip, I break free to grab another condom package.

This time I want to stare into her eyes because fuck it, I'm falling hard.

There's not a damn thing I can do to stop it.

"Can I do it?" She taps my forearm. "Let me put it on you."

I hand the package to her. Watching in rapt wonder, I roll onto my back so she can sheath me.

Her touch is gentle and careful. Her gaze darts from my cock to my face as she rolls the condom on me with a thoughtful touch.

Before I can flip us over, she's on me.

I look away because this is more than I can bear. This much beauty and honesty are enough to shred me.

I bite back a groan when she guides me to her.

I stare at our bodies as she slides onto my cock, inch by inch.

Her back bows, her hands fall to my chest, and she rides me with wild abandon, using my body to give her all the pleasure she needs.

***

I tie the sash on Bianca's dress into a tight bow. "You're sure you need to leave?"

Her hands drop to cover mine. "I'm sure."

I'm far from grateful that this night is coming to an end. I wanted more. I anticipated more, but she needs space, so I'm not going to get in the way of that.

"I need something from you before you go."

Her head darts up. "I'm too sore for more."

Leaning forward, I plant a kiss in the middle of her forehead. "I want your number, Bianca."

She reaches to touch my chin. "Do you promise you won't text me the stats of any players on the Mets roster?"

I cross my arms over my chest. "I can't promise that."

The corners of her lips edge up to a grin. "No number then."

I raise a hand as if I'm making a solemn vow. "I promise to keep the stats of the best players in the majors to a minimum."

"I can live with that. Where's your phone?"

I tug it out of the front pocket of my pants. Skimming my fingers over the screen, I pull up my contact list. "Fire away."

She recites her number, watching as I key it into my phone next to her name.

"Send me a text."

I glance up at her. "What?"

"Send me a text so I have your number too."

The last time a woman demanded that from me, I could tell it was a test. She admitted as much when she accused me of keying her number into my phone wrong. I didn't. I had every intention of calling her until that moment.

I thumb out a simple text to Bianca and press send.

Her gaze drops to the phone in her hand when it chimes. She lets out a light laugh before she reads my text aloud. “Kiss me, Bianca.”

“Now,” I say, stepping closer to her.

She does. She wraps a hand around my neck to tug me closer before she presses her sweet, full lips to mine.

Chapter 30

Bianca

"Why are you smiling like that?" My sister circles her finger in front of my face.

I shove another mouthful of pasta into my mouth. After I chew and swallow, I finally answer. "Eat your dinner, and you'll know why."

She points at her plate. "I'm almost done. I admit the food is great, but you've never been this happy because of ravioli before."

Picking up the water glass in front of me, I take a small sip. "Work is going well."

She eyes me skeptically. "Did you meet someone, Bianca?"

"Like who?"

Piercing a piece of ravioli with her fork, she drags it through the delicious tomato sauce. "A man."

I glance over to where the restaurant's owner, Martina Calvetti, is tending to a customer. "Do you think we should ask Marti to recommend something for dessert?"

Vivi's head shakes. "No. I think you should answer my question."

"I meet a lot of men," I say with a sly grin. "Today I met a guy on a job site. He has sixteen children. Sixteen, as in one six."

"You're avoiding my question."

I am, and it's for a very good reason. Vivi can't keep a secret. She's never been able to. If I tell her about Roman, my mom and Thurston will know before this day is over.

When they found out I was dating Kieran, they demanded to meet him. That turned into an inquisition. My mom tossed questions at him about his intentions and how many children he wanted.

It was intense and unnecessary since I didn't see a long-term future with him even back then.

I want what I have with Roman to stay between us for now.

I reach for my sister's hand. "If things ever get serious between a guy and me, you'll be the first to know."

She tilts her head. "Promise?"

Nodding, I point at the food left on her plate. "Finish that so we can grab dessert and go."

She pushes the plate to the side. "Where? I'm not dressed for anything fancy."

"You look beautiful," Marti Calvetti says as she approaches us. "Look at you."

Vivi glances down at the ripped jeans and pink sweater she's wearing. "I'm a mess."

Clucking her tongue, Marti adamantly shakes her head. "You're a beautiful young woman. My grandson would think so too."

I laugh because there are more than a handful of Marti's grandsons in Manhattan. Arietta, a friend of Maren's and an acquaintance of mine, is engaged to one of them. He's the second oldest grandson, Dominick.

"What's his name?" Vivi asks.

"Dante. Dante Calvetti. He's my Robbie's youngest son."

"Dante Calvetti," Vivi repeats. "It has a nice ring to it."

"He's a nice man." Marti's eyebrows perk before she turns her attention to me. "What about you? Is there a man in your life?"

"There's a lot of work in my life," I joke. "I just got a huge promotion."

"That calls for a celebration." Marti claps her hands together. "Dessert is on me."

"You don't have to do that," I say.

"I do so." She squeezes my forearm. "A promotion should be celebrated with something decadent. Tiramisu for both of you."

As soon as she's left the table, my sister has her phone in her palm. Her eyes widen as her fingers skirt over the screen. "I think I'm in love."

Chuckling, I lean forward. "What?"

She flips the screen around to show me an image on Instagram of a handsome man with striking blue eyes, brown hair, and a smile that could light all of New York City. "That's Dante Calvetti."

I lean back in my chair. "Ask Marti to set you up with him."

Closing the browser on her phone, she sighs. "I can't. I'm just like you. It's all work and no fun for me until the end of wedding season."

"There's an end to wedding season?"

She laughs. "Come to think of it, no, so I guess I'm going to end up like you."

My hand darts to my chest as I hold back a laugh. "Like me?"

"Twenty-seven and married to the job with no love life to speak of."

Little does she know that I had the best sex of my life a few nights ago, and since then, I haven't stopped thinking about Roman.

"You'll make time for love," I assure her. "When the right guy comes along, everything will fall into place."

"For you too," she says. "Our men are out there. We're bound to find them one day."

Something deep inside of me feels as though I've found the perfect man for me in Roman. That might just be the sex talking or my infatuation with him taking over my common sense, but I'm going to enjoy my time with him however long it lasts.

***

"I told you I'm not dressed to go anywhere." Vivi tugs on my arm as soon as we step out of Calvetti's. "If you want to go to a club, I need to run home and change."

I motion to the jeans and blue and white striped blouse I'm wearing. "Do I look like I'm ready to party?"

Still holding onto me, she takes a step back. "You look perfect."

Only my sister would tell me that. Work was a full-on disaster today. I spent much of it on a job site with an irate contractor. It started to rain mid-morning, so the white pants I was wearing became a muddy shade of brown from the knees down.

I showered quickly after work, put on the first things I grabbed out of my closet, and ran to meet my sister. I didn't even bother with make-up or a minute for my hair. It's wavy and messy.

"You know that's not true," I point out.

She shakes her head. "Where do you want to go now?"

It's a spot I never visit alone. I only need to say one word, and my sister will know. She always does. "There."

Her eyes latch onto mine. With a slight quiver of her bottom lip, she tugs me even closer to her. "Let's go."

We walk side-by-side, headed to a place only we know. It's the one spot in this crowded city that brings me the most comfort. Tonight, after the day I had, I need it.

Chapter 31

Roman

A two-word text from Bianca brought me to this barstool this Tuesday afternoon.

Rolly's now?

I was powerless to refuse because I've been longing to see her since we said goodbye on Friday night.

She hasn't left my mind once.

The kiss, the fuck, all of it was incredible.

I hear the door to the pub open, so I stand and turn.

I know she's there before I spot her behind a man who just entered. Bianca's dressed in white slacks and a navy blue blouse. Her hair is pinned up. She's absolutely gorgeous as always.

The smile on her face widens when she spots me.

As soon as she's near enough, I reach out a hand to her. My fucking heart is hammering inside my chest again. I'm not surprised. I'm like a kid with his first crush on a girl, except in my case, she's a brilliant woman.

"Thank you for coming," she says softly before she brushes her lips against mine. "I'm between meetings."

I pushed aside an important one to come here. Chad rescheduled it for tomorrow. The client can wait. My need to see Bianca couldn't.

I wait until she's seated before I drop my ass back on the barstool.

Her gaze darts from my face to the glass of sparkling water in front of me. She doesn't seem surprised that I'm not nursing my usual. Bourbon has a place and time in my life. Today, I need a clear mind, so water it is.

Rolly approaches with a lopsided grin on his face.

"Can I get a water too, please?" Bianca requests. "With two lime wedges."

He pats her hand before he takes off.

I turn on the stool so I can face her. "Is everything all right?"

She smiles. "Work is a lot, but I'm good. I'm really good. You?"

"Better now," I say honestly. "I was hoping to see you today, tonight, tomorrow, your pick."

Tucking a loose strand of her hair behind her ear, she laughs. "I wish I could pick all, but I'm busy until Thursday night."

Fuck.

That's two days away.

"Thursday works for me." Even if it didn't, I'd make it work. "Do you want to grab dinner somewhere?"

Before we go to my former residence to fuck.

I leave that out because I hope it's implied. After the night we had, I sense she's going to want more just as much as I do.

"I'd like to cook for you."

I study her face. "You want to cook for me?"

She nods. "I'm a good cook. I don't do it as often as I'd like, but I'd like to make something for us."

"At your apartment?" I question.

"No, in the middle of Times Square on a hotplate," she deadpans.

I huff out a laugh just as Rolly deposits her glass of water on a napkin in front of her.

"Thanks, Rolly," she says with a genuine smile before he walks away.

I tap her forearm to draw her attention back to me. "I'd love to come to your place for dinner."

"You'll bring wine and condoms?"

I look to where Rolly is standing, but he doesn't react.

Bianca leans closer. "I haven't picked up any condoms recently, and I didn't recognize the brand you had the other night, so I thought you might want to bring your own."

I fucking love the fact that she's this comfortable talking about sex with me. "I can handle that."

She drags her tongue over her bottom lip after swallowing a mouthful of water. "Good. I'll text you my address."

I reach for her hand to cover it with mine. "I'm honored that you want me in your home, Bianca."

Staring into my eyes, she sighs. "I like hanging out with you. Cooking dinner feels like it'll be fun. I'll put you to work chopping something. I saw you in the kitchen at Lise. Were you doing some prep work?"

Hell, no. I was downing a glass of wine to calm my goddamn nerves.

"I can chop a carrot," I admit. "You won't believe how well I scramble eggs."

My culinary skills reach far beyond the basics, but that's a discussion for another time.

"Carrots and eggs?" Her nose scrunches. "If you're preparing those at the same time, having Annalise handle the chef duties at the bistro was the right call."

I bite my bottom lip. "That sounded like an insult."

She leans closer, her eyes trained to my mouth. "It was an observation."

"You're hot as fuck," I whisper. "Now, that's an observation."

"So are you." Her eyes gleam. "I know what's under that suit now, so to say I'm a little excited being this close to you is an understatement."

My gaze drops to her lap. "You want me."

"Desperately," she admits.

I take a chance and kiss her softly. "I'm available for a fuck anytime, Bianca."

"Anytime?" she questions with another soft kiss to my lips. "I'll keep that in mind when I'm in bed at night tossing and turning because I'm thinking about you."

I close my eyes because my cock is hardening, and there's nothing I can do to stop it. "I'm a phone call away."

Running the pad of her thumb over my bottom lip, she sighs. "Open your eyes, Roman."

I do, and the sight in front of me steals the breath from my lungs.

Her lips are parted, her eyelids heavy, and her breathing stuttered. She leans closer until her lips brush against my earlobe. "I can't wait to suck you off on Thursday."

It takes every ounce of strength I have not to groan aloud. "Bianca."

One last kiss is all I get before she slides off the barstool, runs a hand over my shoulder, and walks away.

I tap the top of the bar. "Rolly, I'm going to need that drink after all. Make it a double."

Chapter 32

Bianca

I had to run back to the market twice to get everything I needed to cook dinner tonight. I'm not using a recipe. This is more from memory. It's a lamb dish that Maren made for me once while I sat and watched her.

I called her an hour ago to ask what spices I needed for the dry rub for the lamb chops. Before she listed them, she bombarded me with questions about why I was cooking a dish like that for myself.

I laughed it off and told her I was tired of take-out.

After that, she insisted that I make time next week to have dinner at her place with her and Keats. I agreed. It was enough to quiet the questions about why I'm preparing a lamb, rice pilaf, and Greek salad feast for myself.

I take a step back from the stove and inhale deeply.

Everything smells good. I take that as a great sign.

Just as I'm about to grab the dishes to set the table, there's a knock at my door.

I gave Lester a heads-up earlier that I was expecting a guest tonight.

He had his own questions about that, so I slipped him a twenty dollar bill and told him to bring Roman up to my apartment as soon as he arrived. I added an extra ten when he agreed to forget that we had that conversation.

I have no idea if he'd tell Sabrina about my visitor, but since I'm meeting up with her tomorrow, I can fill her in myself.

I wipe my hands on a kitchen towel before I check my outfit one last time.

It's simple.

Jeans and a black short-sleeve sweater.

My feet are bare, and my make-up is minimal. I went for mascara and light pink lipstick. I've caught enough sun lately to give my skin a natural glow.

I pad across the floor, taking deep breaths as I do.

When I reach the door, I close my eyes and wish for the best. It's a simple thing I often saw my father do before he died.

It's calming.

I swing open the door to find Lester with a smile on his face. Roman is directly behind him.

"Mr. Hawthorne has arrived," Lester announces with an outstretched hand that's in search of yet another tip.

I swat it for a low five. "Thanks."

Roman works to hold in a laugh. "Thank you for the company on the ride up, Lester."

Lester's gaze volleys between Roman and me. "I suppose I'll go now?"

"Bye." I wave a few fingers in the air. "Enjoy the rest of your night."

With a shake of his head, he takes off toward the elevator, leaving me alone with the man I'm about to spend the night with.

***

As soon as Roman is inside my apartment, I start laughing.

He turns around to face me. "Is it my outfit?"

I take a step back and rake him from head-to-toe taking in the jeans and T-shirt he's wearing. "You've never looked better."

He tugs on the bottom of the shirt. "I thought you'd want to see me in this at least once."

The New York Yankees T-shirt I bought him fits him like a glove. It does justice to his muscular arms and broad chest.

"You're only going to wear it this one time?" I pout out my bottom lip. "Is there anything I can do to convince you to wear it again? Just for me?"

He closes the distance between us with a few measured steps. Before I know what's happening, I'm wrapped up in his arms. "I believe we can work something out."

I shiver when his hand traces a path down my back. "After dinner."

He glances over his shoulder toward my kitchen. "If you cooked whatever I'm smelling, you're a better chef than I am."

"There are no carrots involved," I confess. "Or eggs."

His gaze moves to the dining room table. "I see that my delivery arrived."

I hold in a laugh. "It did. Thank you, but there must be at least fifty daisies there, Roman."

He nods. "At least."

I laughed when a delivery person showed up at my door an hour ago. He was trying his best to balance the daisies in a vase in one arm while he held tightly to two paper bags filled with wine.

"Six bottles of wine," I point out. "I need to work tomorrow, so we're drinking only one."

"We'll save the other five for when I come over in the future."

Cocking a brow, I smile. "In the future?"

"We both know this is my first visit here." He moves to kiss me softly on the lips. "I hope it becomes a regular thing."

I do too.

It feels right having him here.

"I'll finish up dinner while you open one bottle of wine." I pop one finger in the air. "Just one."

He closes his eyes and inhales. "Smells like lamb, so a bottle of red it is."

Chapter 33

Roman

I claw at the sheets beneath me, trying to keep my hands from reaching out to Bianca.

She ordered me to stop after she hovered her beautiful pussy over my face. It was pure fucking torture.

I couldn't resist, so I tugged her closer and ran my tongue along the seam of her core.

That drew a moan from her as my cock slid out of her mouth.

I went at her like a starving man until she came against my lips. Moments later, she shifted until she was just out of reach. It was then that my cock became her focus. Fuck me, this woman knows how to bring me to the edge.

"Jesus," I grit out through clenched teeth. "So fucking deep."

She's swallowed me, toying at me with her tongue, her lips, and her hands.

I arch my back when her hand drops to the base of my cock.

She squeezes me hard.

"Fuck," I spit out. "I'm going to come."

Her head bobs up and down as she kneels on the bed. Her tits bounce with each movement.

"Bianca." Her name escapes me in a growl. "Let me touch you."

My cock slides out of her mouth. "I want this. It feels so good."

My head falls back on the bed. I twist beneath her. "I'm close."

I expect her to pull back, but she ups the pace. Her strokes are faster, her moans louder. The hum coming from her vibrates through me.

I feel the heat of the orgasm as it sparks at the base of my spine.

I call out, chanting her name over and over as I come with an intensity that leaves her squirming as she swallows all of my release.

***

I tie off the condom and toss it in a wastebasket in her bathroom.

I needed ten minutes after she blew me before I was ready to go again. I surprised myself with that. Bianca, more so. She eagerly crawled over me again, fucking me with a need that I could feel and see.

Her head flew back, she moaned, and as she let herself go, I clung to her thighs, wanting to keep her there forever.

I stare at myself in the mirror that hangs over the sink.

My hair is a fucking mess. My cheeks are red, and there's a small bite mark on my shoulder.

Her teeth landed there when she came.

She fell onto me as she rode me through her orgasm.

The pain from the bite was enough to drive me to fuck her harder. I flipped us over, thrust into her again and again until I blew my load.

My hands fall to the counter as I try and catch my breath.

I don't know what the hell I'm doing anymore. I've always been so careful. I fuck without thinking too far into the future.

I'm not a one-night stand type of guy. I've had a series of short monogamous relationships, but I've never felt anything close to this.

I turn quickly, not wanting to face myself.

I'm fucking up.

A man can't live in two separate worlds for long. Eventually, they have to collide.

A soft knock at the door draws my gaze back up. I scrub a hand over my face. "Bianca," I call out to her. "Come in. I'm decent."

She swings open the door and laughs aloud when she sees me leaning against her bathroom counter with nothing on.

"You're naked," she points out. "That's decent?"

"You're naked too." My hand drops to the base of my cock. "That's perfect."

She moves closer half a step. "Your phone was ringing. I think it's still in the pocket of your jeans."

A call this late at night is never good news. "I need to check that."

She moves to the side as I breeze past her and stalk toward her bed. My jeans are on the floor in a crumpled mess next to the T-shirt I was wearing.

I tug my phone free and scan the screen. Three missed calls and two text messages.

I run through them quickly, noting that all are from the same number.

"It's a client's daughter," I say softly. "My client died an hour ago."

I hear Bianca's footsteps behind me. "I'm sorry."

I'm relieved.

When I grabbed my phone, I expected the missed calls to be personal. "She was very sick."

"Do you need to go?"

There's little I can do at this time of night for my client's daughter, but I'm needed somewhere else. I belong here with Bianca as much as I belong at home.

I turn to face her. "I should."

Her hands drop in front of her. "I understand."

I stand there, staring at every inch of her. "Tonight was…"

"The first of many?" she questions. "You'll come back again soon?"

"I will," I whisper because there's no fucking way I'm going to have the strength to end this as I've done with women in the past. "I'm having dinner with a client tomorrow, so how about I drop by on Saturday night?"

"I'd like that." She smiles. "Do you want me to order you an Uber?"

I'm in no rush. There's no one waiting up for me. I won't contact my client's daughter until tomorrow morning. "Thank you, but I've got it covered."

I plan to walk home.

That will give me what I need most right now.

Time. I need time to think about how the future I've always seen for myself looks different now because I want Bianca in it.

Chapter 34

Bianca

"You cooked dinner for Roman last night?" Sabrina raises a brow as we stroll down a street on the Upper East Side. "It's serious, isn't it?"

I tug the white cardigan I'm wearing closer to my body to ward off the evening wind that's picked up since we left Crispy Biscuit. "I like him."

Sabrina smiles. "A lot."

"Yes," I admit as we slow to a stop to wait for a crossing light. "He's fun. We have a great time together."

Her gaze darts around to the people gathering near us. "How is the sex?"

I'm grateful she asked it in an almost whisper. Rolling my eyes, I jerk a thumb over my shoulder.

She shakes her head. "No one is listening to our conversation."

"I am."

We turn in unison to see a woman with gray hair standing behind us. She's wearing a light blue blouse with a white bow at the collar. Purple-rimmed eyeglasses sit atop her nose.

"Excuse me?" Sabrina huffs out a laugh.

"I don't get out as much as I used to." The woman shrugs. "I'll take any excitement I can get, even if that means eavesdropping on the conversation of two beautiful young women."

I smile at her before my gaze darts to Sabrina. I find her with a wide grin on her face.

"So tell me." The woman behind us taps the center of my back. "How was the sex?"

"Phenomenal," I admit.

"I miss that." The woman squeezes my shoulder. "Hold onto him as long as you can because not all sex is not great sex."

She moves around us as the light turns.

Watching her walk away, Sabrina and I both launch into a giggling fit.

"That just happened," she manages between laughs. "You just told a stranger that Roman Hawthorne is a beast in bed."

Calming myself, I hold a hand against my stomach. "I wasn't lying. It was epic."

She reaches out to grab my hand. "I have to agree with whoever that woman was. Hold onto him, Bianca. Men like that aren't easy to find."

***

Fifteen minutes later, we're standing on the sidewalk staring up at a townhouse.

"Give me your first thoughts," I say to my cousin.

"The brick isn't in good shape." She sighs. "That's expensive to replace."

I nod. "You're right, but the location is stellar."

She taps a finger against her lips. "The offer to work with me still stands. I know what you do at Packton is a hell of a lot different than what I do, but I could use your insight to help me grow my business."

My knowledge in the building sector is increasing by the day, but I love my job. "When do you tour the inside?"

"Monday morning. I thought I'd take the weekend to think more about it and to grab a peek at the exterior. Thanks for tagging along for that."

I'd offer to tour the interior with her on Monday, but my day is booked solid. "You're considering it though. I can tell."

Her gaze darts to me. "How can you tell?"

"You tap your lip whenever you're leaning toward agreeing to something." I demonstrate by tapping my lips with my index finger. "You did the same thing earlier when I suggested we take the subway here instead of an Uber."

Her hand immediately drops. "I'm that transparent?"

"You're that adorable."

She laughs that off. "Let's go grab a drink so I can think more about it."

I reach up to tap my lip again. "I'll think about that."

My hand is in hers in an instant. "Hilarious, Bianca. There's a bar around the corner that serves a killer martini."

"Lead the way."

We start in the direction we just came from, with me following closely on her heel.

I wish I had worn something other than jeans, a tour T-shirt from my favorite band, and the cardigan. I pulled an old pair of black leather boots out of my closet before I left home. They have withstood thousands of trips on foot around Manhattan.

Sabrina's outfit is as cute as she is. It's a red dress, a short denim jacket, and a pair of low-heeled red sandals.

With my hair in a messy bun on top of my head, I look like I just rolled out of bed, or I'm ready to drop into one for a good eight hours of sleep.

Once we round a corner, Sabrina's finger darts out in the air. "It's just ahead. They always have live music."

I can hear the soft sounds of a guitar coming from the open doorway.

Suddenly, it's drowned out by the sharp bite of a cell phone ringing. Sabrina curses under her breath. "Dammit, that's me."

We slow to a stall as she tugs the phone out of her purse. "I need to take this. It's the manager of one of my buildings. We're having an issue with some of the air conditioning units."

"I'll go ahead, grab us a table, and order two martinis."

She nods her approval before she swipes a finger across her phone's screen and answers the call the way she always does. "This is Sabrina. I hope you're having a great day."

I leave her there while I take the last few steps to the bar at a leisurely pace.

I look over the exterior façade. It's gorgeous. The glass doors are framed in dark wood. That same wood carries around four large windows.

I glance into one wanting a sneak peek into the interior.

I'm not disappointed. A large wooden bar sits to the right. To the left is a collection of round tables with sleek silver chairs.

A woman is playing a guitar near the doorway. The music is soothing, adding to the ambiance of the place.

The crowd inside is thin, but I want to get settled before Sabrina joins me.

I take a step toward the bar, but I freeze instantly because I can't believe what I'm seeing.

The man I slept with last night is sitting at the bar.

His hands are all over a blonde. He's running his fingers over the thigh of her jeans. The other is caressing a path over her shoulder.

Time stalls and my heart skips a beat when he leans forward and whispers something to her. I move slowly until I have a clearer view of them from the side so I can see what happens next.

It's a kiss.

It's not sweet. There's nothing soft about it.

I catch a clear view of a passionate embrace between Roman and someone who isn't me.

Chapter 35

Bianca

I glance at the doorway in search of Sabrina, but she's not there. I need an anchor. I feel like I'm floating in disbelief at the moment as I watch Roman kiss the blonde like he can't wait to get her into bed.

His hollow words about only fucking one woman at a time ring in my head.

He fucked me last night, and we didn't talk or text at all today, so unless I missed an imaginary conversation he had with me, he's a liar.

He's going to take this woman to bed tonight.

The way he's kissing her is a sign of that. Not to mention the fact that her hands are now running all over his thighs.

She's burning a path over his jeans with her fingers, just stopping short of grabbing his cock through the denim.

I take a step toward them, and one of her hands darts to the front of the T-shirt he's wearing. The other fists the lapel of his dark gray suit jacket.

She looks like she's ready to hop into his lap right here and right now.

He scoops a hand around the back of her head to guide her so he can deepen the kiss.

It's an intimate move he's made with me.

I can't believe what's happening right in front of me.

Rage runs through me as I stalk toward them.

I didn't feel like this when I caught Kieran slamming his dick into Ulla. This is splitting me in two. Tears are about to spill out of my eyes, but I hold them back.

I won't let him see me cry.

I catch sight of Sabrina coming through the doorway just as I'm next to Roman.

"This is quite the business meeting."

My voice tears the lovers apart. The woman is the first to look at me. Roman glances down before he looks in my direction.

His already full lips are swollen from the kiss. He's sporting more stubble than he normally does, and his hair is messier than usual.

"You said you had a business meeting," I say to him.

"That was hours ago," the woman responds. "Are you my new assistant? I know we spoke on the phone earlier, but you said you couldn't meet up tonight. I thought we agreed that I'd see you at my office on Monday morning unless you want to come with me tomorrow while I look for an apartment. I'm still learning how to navigate Manhattan."

Shaking my head, I stare at her. "What?"

"What's going on?" Sabrina moves to stand next to me. "Do you need help?"

"I could use another drink." The blonde woman laughs. "It's suddenly very hot in here, if you know what I mean."

I shake my head, not wanting to join in as she laughs. Roman, on the other hand, lets out a deep chuckle.

"You're hot too?" I point a finger at him. "Did kissing her make you all hot and bothered?"

The corners of his lips curve up as he lifts a shoulder in a shrug.

Is he fucking serious right now?

The rage I'm feeling morphs into sadness, disappointment, or maybe it's regret.

Whatever it is, it drives me to pick up the glass in front of him, turn to him, and with a snap of my wrist, I toss the clear liquid at him before I slam the glass down on the bar. "Go to hell."

Just as I turn to walk away, his hand grabs ahold of my wrist. "Wait."

I stop in place. "For what?"

He lets go of me and moves to stand. Sliding a hand over his face to brush off what's left of his drink, he looks down at me. "Bianca, right?"

I stare at his lips because that's not how my name usually sounds when he says it. His voice is different. It's deeper and rougher.

I take a step back when he removes his suit jacket, and I see his bare arms.

"Wh…what…what's happening?" I stutter out as I look at the intricate black and gray tattoo that wraps around his right bicep.

"I'm Matt." He shoves his hand at me. "Matt Hawthorne."

Chapter 36

Bianca

"You're not Roman?" That question leaves me without any thought as I take his hand in mine for a quick shake.

"I'm Matt." The man standing in front of me nods. "Roman's twin brother."

"Twins?" The blonde woman Matt was kissing jumps off her barstool. "Are you serious? There's another man in this city that looks like you?"

He turns to her. "We're identical."

"I knew transferring here from Seattle was the right move." She waves a hand in front of her face. "The two of you together must be a sight for sore eyes."

Matt huffs out a laugh. "I've got my hands full here, so…"

"Right." She gathers up her purse. "I'm staying at the Bishop Hotel in Tribeca. Room 301. Stop by if you want to finish what we started."

"Thanks for the invitation…" his voice trails.

"Paisley," she stresses. "You forgot my name?"

"I blame it on temporary trauma." He dabs the front of his wet T-shirt with a napkin. "It's not every day that a glass of water is thrown at me."

I wince. "I'm so sorry."

He laughs it off. "It's not a big deal."

"It's kind of a big deal," Paisley chimes in. "We had something pretty special going on before we were rudely interrupted."

"Maybe that's all it was meant to be." Matt pats another napkin against the lapel of the suit jacket in his hand. "I'm going to be tied up for the rest of the night."

Paisley steps closer to him. "I could do that for real. My ex-husband taught me how to tie a knot that is impossible to escape from."

Matt's eyes widen. "Hard pass, Presley."

"Paisley," she corrects him. "My offer stands. Room 301. Bishop Hotel Tribeca."

He flashes her a smile.

Sabrina, Matt, and I all watch her walk away.

He turns to face me. "Roman's told me a lot about you, but he forgot to mention that you have perfect aim."

Sabrina laughs. "It did hit you dead center in the face."

"Dead center," he agrees. "You overheard who I am, so who are you?"

"Sabrina Marks," she says, offering her hand. "Bianca's cousin."

His hand falls in hers for a quick shake. "It's a pleasure to meet you."

"I'm sorry," I say again. "I had no idea that Roman has a brother."

"Brothers," he corrects me as he slides his suit jacket back on. "We have a younger brother and a sister too."

Roman and I haven't discussed our families. He assumes I'm Thurston Marks's daughter, but that's the extent of the exploration of our family trees.

"Four kids?" Sabrina asks. "Your parents are brave. I'm an only child."

The sound of a phone ringing interrupts us. I look to Sabrina, but she points at Matt. "It must be you."

He tugs a phone from his suit jacket. "It's Rome."

My heart skips a beat at the mention of his name.

With a perk of his brow, and his eyes pinned on me, Matt answers the call. "Hey, you're never going to guess who I'm standing next to right now."

I glance at Sabrina, but she's staring at a blond-haired guy sitting at the end of the bar.

"It's Bianca." Matt chuckles. "She threw a drink at me meant for you, so the next time I see you I'm passing that along. Be prepared to get a bucket of ice water in the…"

His voice trails.

"I was with a woman." He smiles. "I'll see you tomorrow morning. Spread some goodnight kisses around for me."

Sabrina and I glance at each other as he ends the call.

"Rome got a good chuckle out of that." He pats his chest. "The last time someone mistook me for him, they bombarded me with legal talk about heirs and annuities. This was a hell of a lot more interesting than that."

Sabrina and I laugh in unison.

His gaze drops to his phone when it starts ringing again. He answers it immediately. "Dr. Hawthorne."

I turn to the side when I feel my phone vibrate in the pocket of my jeans. I slide it out and read the text message that just arrived.

Roman: ***So you met my double tonight? It sounds like it was memorable.***

Smiling, I text him back as Matt continues speaking to someone about an eye injury.

Bianca: ***You're much more handsome than he is.***

"Did you know he had a twin?" Sabrina shakes her head. "Of course, you didn't know. I saw how angry you were when you tossed that drink at him."

I glance at her. "I thought it was Roman."

"Me too," she admits. "I'm glad it wasn't."

"Me too," I repeat her words. "I think I might skip the drink and call it a night."

She reaches down to squeeze my hand. "An old friend is sitting at the bar. I'm going to join him and catch up."

I look at the handsome man who can't stop staring at my cousin. "Old friend or old more than a friend?"

"Old college friend," she clarifies. "I haven't seen him in years. Make time to catch up with me next week."

"I will," I say just as my phone starts ringing.

I glance down to see Roman's name on the screen. I answer immediately. "Hey."

"Hey you," he says in his sexy-as-hell voice. "I'm sorry I'm not there."

"Me too," I admit. "Your brother is a dead ringer for you."

"That's what I've heard," he jokes.

"I'm going to head home," I say softly as I glance to where Matt is standing near the bar, still talking on the phone. "I heard your brother tell you to spread some goodnight kisses around."

He lets out a low chuckle. "That started when we were kids. My mom spread a lot of goodnight kisses around with her brood. There are four of us in total."

"I hope you'll save a few of those kisses for me for tomorrow."

"You know I will," he growls. "I'll plant them wherever you want them."

A shiver runs through me. "I'll hold you to that."

"You better." He lets out a low groan. "Get home safely, Bianca."

"I will," I say before I end the call.

I feel a tap on my shoulder. I turn to find Matt.

I may not have noticed it at first, but I can tell that he's not Roman. The way he looks at me is different. The left side of his mouth isn't quite the same shape as Roman's when he smiles, as he is now.

"Roman wanted us to meet soon." He shoves his phone back into his pocket. "You're incredibly important to him."

That surprises me. I'm sure it shows in my expression. "Really?"

"He talks about you all the time."

"All good things, I hope," I mumble nervously.

He steps closer to me. "I'm glad he found you, Bianca. You're good to him. He needs that."

"I need it too," I admit.

"I'm on call tonight, and there's a poodle emergency, so I need to run." He moves to step around me. "I'm sure I'll be seeing a lot more of you."

I watch him sprint away, relieved that I didn't actually see the man I'm falling in love with in another woman's arms tonight.

Chapter 37

Roman

I toss the keys in my hand on the foyer table and stalk across the open concept apartment until I reach the granite kitchen counter. I drop the tray holding two coffees on it, along with the box containing six cupcakes.

I'm on my way home from Sweet Bluebells, a bakery I've been frequenting for years. I'm making this short pit stop because I do so almost every Saturday morning.

"Matthew!" I yell toward the hallway that leads to his bedroom. "Time to rise and shine."

If there were a woman here, I wouldn't be.

My brother always drops me a warning text if he's bringing a woman home. It's not because I keep close tabs on him, but we live in the same building, three floors apart.

I stop by unannounced just as often as he does at my place. We share keys, and meals and Matt helps me out whenever I need it.

"I'm awake," he calls from behind his closed bedroom door. "I'm looking for pants."

Tugging one of the coffees free from the cupboard tray, I laugh. "I'll wait."

As soon as the words leave my mouth, I hear his bare feet on the hardwood in the hallway.

He rounds the corner in gray sweatpants.

"You look like you haven't slept a wink."

Raking a hand through his hair, he heads straight for the coffee. "Eye surgery on a poodle last night. I got home two, maybe three hours ago."

"Shit." I pop open the pastry box. "I can take off."

He glances at the cupcakes. "Which one is mine?"

I point at one with rich chocolate icing and a candy heart on top. "That one."

"True love," he reads the words etched on the heart. "I thought that was Bianca."

Our eyes lock. "You didn't tell her, did you?"

He goes in for a bite of the cupcake, taking half of it in his mouth. Chewing, he studies my face. Once he's swallowed, he smiles. "What? That you're falling in love with her?"

That's a confession I made to him the night I walked home from Bianca's apartment. Matt was on his way in after a long day at work. I was floating on cloud nine. He noticed.

I let everything spill out, including the fact that I'm crazy about her.

"You kept that to yourself," I say.

"Why do I get the impression that you're keeping a lot to yourself?" he counters. "She didn't know about me. I doubt like hell she knows about Callum or Delia."

I shake my head at the mention of our siblings. "I talked briefly about Delia."

Matt cracks a grin. "She's your favorite, so that makes sense."

"No comment."

He finishes the cupcake in one bite. "Bianca doesn't know anything else?"

Hanging my head, I sigh. "It's moving fast, Matt. We've gone from having fun to me falling for her."

"Judging by what happened last night, she's head over heels for you."

I glance at him. "Why would you say that?"

He scoops up his coffee cup. "The look in her eyes cut straight through me. There was so much pain there, Rome. She saw me kissing the woman I met at the bar, and it broke her."

"Because she thought it was me," I whisper.

"She didn't know I exist, so yeah." He takes a sip of coffee. "She walked in, saw that, and tossed a glass of water at me."

I shouldn't take comfort in that, but I do. Bianca's reaction wouldn't have been so swift and strong if what she felt for me wasn't serious.

"You need to tell her everything, Rome."

"I've never…"

"I know," he interrupts. "You've never let a woman get this close to you before. I get it, but this is different."

"It's a lot to throw at her," I say quietly.

"It's two adorable little girls." He jerks his thumb toward a picture hanging on the wall of me with my daughters. "You're a package deal, so clue Bianca into that before she stumbles on the fact that you're a dad."

I look at the image of Dora and Georgie, my two beautiful girls.

"I'll tell her tonight."

"Good." He moves to stand. "Take these cupcakes home before I eat them all. We both know there will be hell to pay if I do that."

I chuckle. "Your nieces will be down here in a flash if I come home without a cupcake for each of them and one for Morena."

Morena Bevins has been helping me with the girls since the day I became a dad. She's more than a nanny. She's a part of our family.

I rented a two-bedroom apartment in the building next door for her. My girls love it because they get to have a sleepover at least a couple of times a month. It works well for Morena too, since her daughter lives two blocks away.

He slams the lid on the box shut. "I'm going to shower, and then it's back to the clinic for me."

"You're working hard."

"Always." He perks a brow. "I wouldn't have it any other way."

"I'll bring the girls by the clinic later."

"Good." He pats my shoulder as he rounds me on his way toward the hallway. "There's a poodle with an eye patch they'll want to meet."

I pick up the box of cupcakes and start toward the door. I'll spend the day with my daughters and the evening with Bianca.

My two worlds are about to collide, and I know that wherever the pieces of my life fall after this, tomorrow, I'll still wake up as the luckiest father on this planet.

Chapter 38

Bianca

I made the worst possible first impression on Matt Hawthorne last night.

Even though I had no idea that Roman has a twin brother, I let my anger drive me. Tossing that glass of water in his face felt amazing at the moment, but afterward, I was hit by a wave of guilt.

As soon as I woke up this morning, I decided I needed to right that wrong.

Matt might have told me that it was fine, but I had to do something to show him that I'm sorry.

While I was drinking my first coffee of the day, I did a quick online search for the doctor.

He's a veterinarian working at Premier Pet Care.

His bio on the clinic's website states that he loves animals and his family. I dove a little deeper into his social media and noticed that he's a fan of Asher Foster. Matt tagged the award-winning singer and songwriter in one of his posts from a few weeks ago.

According to the caption of a very sad faced selfie taken by Matt and another vet named Donovan Hunt, they didn't get tickets to Asher's upcoming tour.

Asher's wife, Falon, did some photography work for Packton last month. I had the chance to meet her and pamper her with her favorite foods as she spent the better part of three days in one of our new properties taking shots that will be used for the marketing campaign by our sales force.

It wasn't my place to step in and make sure she was adequately fed. Still, when I stumbled on her photographing a suite in the luxury condo building we're set to open later this year, I saw a sad selection of sandwiches and a wilted salad on a table.

When I had more food brought in, she thanked me and offered to help me if she ever could.

I called in that favor an hour ago.

Not only will Matt Hawthorne be backstage at Asher's concert in Brooklyn this summer, but he'll be meeting the artist too. He's free to bring along a guest of his choosing.

Falon emailed me a personalized invitation from Asher himself twenty minutes ago, so I printed it off, tucked it into an envelope, and I'm headed to the vet clinic to drop it off.

I'm hoping it's open so I can leave it at the reception desk for him. If not, I'll give it to Roman when I see him tonight so he can hand deliver it to his brother.

I round the corner on the approach to the vet clinic. I chose to wear flat sandals, a pair of white shorts and a long-sleeved pink blouse. I piled my hair into a messy up-do. I'll jump in the shower after grabbing some lunch.

I want to pamper myself before I see Roman tonight.

We haven't discussed when he'll come over later, but I'll text him late this afternoon to see what his schedule is.

I tug on the handle of the door of the vet clinic.

To my surprise, it opens with ease.

I venture inside to the sound of a high-pitched bark. Vivi and I had a dog when we were kids. It was a special part of our childhood and helped us after our dad died. The dog brought us comfort during some of the most challenging days of our lives.

I stalk toward the reception desk to find a pretty blonde dressed in blue scrubs behind it. She greets me with an open-mouthed smile. "Welcome to Premier Pet Care. What can I do for you today?"

I glance toward the waiting room filled with people holding leashes attached to dogs and carriers containing furry creatures. I spot the sweet face of an orange-haired cat in one. "I have something for Dr. Hawthorne. Can I leave it with you?"

I tug the envelope containing Asher's note from the tote bag slung over my shoulder and push it toward her.

"He's here today," she says with a lilt in her tone. "He should be done with his patient shortly. If you want to give it to him yourself, I can make that happen."

I wasn't expecting to see Roman's brother, but it does give me the opportunity to apologize again.

"If it's not a bother, that would be great."

She picks up the receiver of the desk phone in front of her and taps a button. "Dr. Hawthorne, there's someone here to see you."

As she pauses, she glances at me. "No, it's not them. It's a woman, named…"

"Bianca," I whisper.

She repeats my name, ends the call, and glances at me. "He'll be right here."

I take a deep breath. "Thank you."

My attention is drawn to the waiting room again when a dog starts howling. Laughter erupts as a man sitting with a small puppy on his lap comments that he feels the same way whenever he has to go to his doctor.

"Bianca?"

I turn around at the sound of Matt's voice behind me. He's dressed in jeans and a black polo shirt. A white lab coat covers that. *Dr. Matthew Hawthorne* is stitched across it on the left side of his chest.

"Matt," I say his name softly. "I'm sorry to bother you."

"Not a bother." He smiles. "What can I do for you?"

I hold out the envelope that I hastily wrote his first name across. "This is a small token of my regret about what happened last night."

The woman behind the reception desk perks a brow, but she doesn't say a word.

He waves my hand away. "That's not necessary. It was a misunderstanding. You thought I was my brother."

I push the envelope at him. "Please accept it."

He takes it from me, opening it quickly. Tugging out the paper, he reads it before he glances up at me. "Are you fucking serious?"

The woman behind the counter lets out a giggle.

"I noticed on Instagram that you're a fan of Asher Foster, so I called in a favor."

He shakes his head. "What the hell? This is too much."

"Does it make up for my mistake last night?"

Laughter erupts from him. "I'd gladly take a glass of water in the face in exchange for this any day of the week."

I glance over my shoulder when I hear another loud bark coming from the waiting room. "I think someone needs your attention. I'm going to take off."

He taps the envelope and the note against his palm. "Thank you, Bianca. This was incredibly thoughtful of you."

I nod in response and turn to leave.

I'm one step closer to the door of the clinic when it flies open and two small girls rush in. They dart around me, headed straight for Matt.

It's all a blur.

I turn back around to see them jumping into his arms as he squats to greet them.

They hug him tightly. One screams his name, "Uncle Matty!"

When they pull back and glance in my direction, I stare at them until I hear a familiar voice behind me. "Bianca?"

As if I'm moving in slow motion, I turn to see Roman standing in the doorway of the clinic.

"We beat you to the door, Daddy," a soft voice says from behind me.

Daddy.

Roman is a dad to beautiful identical twin girls.

Chapter 39

Roman

This can't be happening, but it is.

I'm not dreaming. This isn't a nightmare. It's my reality. The woman I'm falling in love with is standing inches away from the loves of my life.

My daughters and Bianca are all staring at me.

Matt moves to stand. "Why don't I take the girls to the break room?"

Dora, my adventurous little girl, jumps at the chance. She literally jumps up and down. The stuffed bunny in her hand bounces with her. "Buggy is sick. I brought him so you could make him feel better."

Matt runs a hand over the stuffed animal's ears. "Let's take him into an exam room." His gaze shifts to Riona, the vet assistant standing behind the reception desk. "Miss Myerson is going to help us."

Riona nods. As she rounds the desk, she reaches for Georgie's hand. We've been here enough for her to know that my youngest twin, the most sensitive one, needs extra encouragement when it comes to a visit to an exam room.

"We'll be right back," Matt says as he tosses me a look.

He senses I need a moment alone with Bianca. Hell, I need more than that to explain what she just witnessed, what she now knows. I'm a father. I'm a single dad raising two six-year-olds on my own.

I wait until my daughters are out of view before I approach Bianca.

She studies my face. "You're a dad."

I never had this conversation with a woman I've been seeing before. That's because every short-term relationship I've had burned itself out before we got to the '*meet my kids*' stage.

I made a promise to myself when my daughters were infants that I'd be selective about anyone I brought into their orbit. I didn't want them falling in love with a woman I knew I'd never love, so a meet-up never happened.

Until now.

I wanted this. I didn't realize it would happen like this.

"They're so beautiful," she whispers. "How old are they?"

"Six," I answer quickly. "Dora will tell you that they're six-and-a-half, but that's not the case for another two months."

"Dora," she repeats her name.

"And Georgie," I say softly.

Her bottom lip quivers. "Georgie."

I nod. "I was planning on telling you tonight."

Her eyes lock on mine, and I see something swimming in the blue depths. I can't tell if it's shock or sadness.

I have no idea if she sees herself with kids at some point or if the knowledge that I'm a dad is enough to drive her away.

I glance down at her shaking hands. "Bianca, I'm sorry."

She reaches for one of my hands. "Please, no. Don't say that."

I hold onto her, cradling her hand in between mine. "I've always been very protective of them. It's just the three of us."

"Just you three?"

I don't want to talk about this in the middle of a loud vet clinic, but I don't have a goddamn choice because I'm scared that if she walks out of here now, I'll never see her again. "Their mother isn't… she's not a part of their lives. I've been raising them alone since shortly after they were born. They've never met a woman I've been involved with, but this is different. I want you to know them. I really want them to know you, Bianca."

The door to the clinic swings open, and a woman holding tightly to the leash of a Great Dane walks in. She struggles to control the dog as it rushes at me with its tail wagging.

Just as it tries to jump up to greet me, another vet assistant races around the corner.

Bianca looks at me. "I think I should go."

That's the last thing I want, but I sense it's exactly what she needs. My heart is twisting inside my chest, but I nod even though I want to fall to my knees and plead with her to give me more time to explain.

With the Great Dane owner trying to calm her dog, and the vet assistant telling her Matt will see them shortly, I watch Bianca walk out of the clinic.

***

"You're not a fucking mind reader." Matt taps the center of my forehead. "You have no idea what Bianca is thinking, so knock it off."

His gaze bounces between my face and the spot on the waiting room sofa where my two girls are sitting as they pet a dog.

As soon as Matt, Dora and Georgie came storming out of an exam room, I was waiting with a smile.

I can't let my daughters see how torn up I am. I'm their hero. I've always kept my emotions in check in front of them, even when they've asked me repeatedly why they don't have a mommy.

I thought they would, but not everything goes to plan.

"Daddy!" Dora calls from where she's sitting. "Uncle Matty gave Buggy a big band-aid."

I hold back a laugh at the amount of gauze wrapped around the stuffed bunny's head. "He's the best of the best."

Georgie waves an orange balloon animal at me. "He made me this."

"That dog has a hell of a long neck," I say under my breath. "You need to get your eyes checked, old man."

Matt was born ten minutes before me, so he's always been the butt of my jokes.

"It's a giraffe, asshole, " he whispers before he offers me a broad smile. "It's not like you can do any better."

He's right. I can't. I provide everything I can to my daughters so they have a life that's comfortable but not extravagant.

Matt provides just as much love and understanding as I do. The bonus he brings to the table is whatever fun he can dream up.

This month it's balloon animals.

Last month, he used washable markers to create a mural in the girls' playroom that they've been adding to ever since.

I couldn't have been the father that I am without him.

"Can I get one too?" A young brown-haired boy asks as he approaches us. "Can you make me a walrus too, Doctor H?"

I elbow my brother. "Make him a walrus just like the one you made Georgie."

Matt runs a hand over the little guy's head. "You bet. Just give me a minute to finish this conversation."

The little boy's gaze volleys between us. "Is he your clone?"

Matt laughs. "Twin."

The boy shrugs a shoulder before taking off in a sprint back to his father and the dog they brought in.

My brother turns to face me. "Give Bianca a day or two to process everything, then reach out to her."

That was my plan, but I considered cutting the day or two down to a few hours.

"She cares about you." He pats my cheek. "There's no way in hell that I'm wrong about this."

I trust him. I always have, so I'll be as patient as I can while I wait to hear from the only woman I've ever loved.

Chapter 40

Bianca

I sit on the edge of the bed and stare at the photograph in my hands. It's not pristine. The edges are curled, and there's a small rip in one corner. That happened one night years ago when Vivi wouldn't let it go.

We argued, I tugged at it, and at the end of our battle, I had the smallest piece of it in between my fingers, and Vivi had tears streaming down her face.

She's always told me that I'm the lucky one because I have memories of our dad. I do, but they're fading with each passing day.

I used to remember the smell of his cologne, but that's not the case anymore.

I held onto the sound of his voice for as long as I could, but it's been drowned out by time.

I trace a fingertip over my dad's face in the photo. He was handsome with his strong jawline and his dark brown hair. I've always been grateful that I was blessed with the same blue eyes he had.

When I look in the mirror, I'm sometimes hit with the memory of how he used to look at me. It was with pride when I first learned how to ride a two-wheel bike, and it was with sorrow when he told us that our mom had to be in the hospital for an operation.

It was her first step toward healing from cancer, but we were too young to understand any of that.

He was a good dad.

He taught me right from wrong and how to love everyone. He showed me that I'm a strong person and that kindness always wins.

Family meant everything to him, and he took every measure he could to protect us. The one thing he couldn't protect us from his passing. The pain of that was all too real.

He died while he was away on a business trip. It was a heart attack, unexpected and final.

My eyes fill with tears as I think about the last moments of his life. He spent them alone. What thoughts must have crowded his mind before he took his last breath?

I dart to my feet when I hear my front door opening. Swiping a hand over my face, I try to brush away the tears.

"Bianca?" Vivi asks from the other room. "Are you here?"

She'll never learn to call before she barges in, and today I'm extra thankful for that. I drop the photo of my dad onto my bed. "I'm coming."

Before I can get out of my bedroom, my sister appears in the doorway with a small bouquet of daisies in her hand. "I picked these up at the Farmer's Market this morning."

My heart lurches inside my chest, and the tears come again, but this time it's different.

"What's wrong?" Fear taints her tone as she steps closer. "Did something happen?"

I manage a smile. "I'm happy."

Her eyes fill with tears too. "That makes me happy too."

I draw her into my arms for a tight hug. "I think I'm in love."

"What? With who?" She steps back instantly.

"His name is Roman," I say quietly. "Roman Hawthorne."

"Where did you meet him? What's he like?" She brushes away a tear running down her cheek. "Tell me all about him."

"He's a good man." I choke on a sob. "I think he might love me too."

She moves my hair over my shoulder before she pats my cheek. "How could he not love you? You're beautiful. You're smart and so kind. You're the best sister in the world."

I manage a smile. "You are."

"I'm second best." She laughs. "You're the one who has always been there for me. You've taken care of me for a long time."

She's done the same for me. "That's what sisters do."

"Maybe you and Roman will get married and have two daughters like mom and dad did." She leans back. "They'll be best friends just like we are."

I've never considered Vivi my best friend, but that's exactly who she is. We've stumbled through life's challenges together, celebrated next to one another, and we've always cheered each other on.

I take a deep breath. "He has two daughters. Twins."

"Twins?" Her hand darts to her mouth. "Like identical?"

I smile through a new rush of tears. "He's a twin too. He has a twin brother named Matt."

She laughs. "That's wild. What are his daughters' names?"

I reach for her hand to cradle it in mine. "Dora and Georgie."

A single tear streams down her face. "Dora and Georgie."

I nod.

"It's fate," she whispers. "Roman is your person, Bianca."

"It's early," I confess. "I haven't even officially met his daughters yet, but my heart split open when I saw them. They're so beautiful, V."

"Love moves at the pace it wants to." She sighs. "It sweeps in when you least expect it and carries you away to your forever, so enjoy the ride."

Chapter 41

Roman

A knock at my apartment door sends me in that direction, but Georgie beats me to it. Her blue eyes flash with happiness as she breezes past me with the biggest smile on her face.

If I could bottle those smiles and keep them forever, I'd never worry about tomorrow, but I do. My daughters have full lives ahead of them, and I admit I sometimes think about what life will be like when they start dating or how I'll feel on their wedding days.

Georgie swings open the wooden door and squeals in delight. "Kita!"

Nikita Wolf scoops Georgie up and into her arms. "Georgie girl, how are you?"

Everyone in my inner circle can tell the twins apart. Dora is half an inch taller than Georgie, but the dead giveaway is their smiles. Dora's is always wide. It's a sign of the happiness she carries around within her.

Georgie's is softer but just as inviting. The left corner of her lip darts up just a hair more than the right side.

"I'm good," Georgie answers. "You look so pretty."

Nikita smiles. "You do too."

We all turn when we hear the thundering charge of Dora's bare feet on the hardwood. She appears from around the corner that leads to the hallway. A pink ribbon is tied around her head. The frayed end is flopping in front of her right eye.

"What's going on there?" Nikita holds in a laugh.

Dora's hand darts up to show Buggy. "I'm hurt just like Buggy is. A piece of candy would make me feel better."

Nikita's blue eyes search my face. There's an unspoken question there, so I toss her a nod even though the girls had cupcakes this morning before we went to visit Matt at the clinic.

A smile takes over her lips as she gingerly places Georgie down before she yanks two red heart shaped lollipops from the pocket of her jean jacket. "Look what I brought."

The girls scream together.

Dora is the first to rush over with a thank you hug. Georgie joins in as soon as her lollipop is unwrapped.

Nikita tucks a strand of her black hair behind her ear as the girls step back. "I came to see your dad. I need to talk to him for a minute."

That perks my brow. "About?"

She elbows me. "Something that will make you happy."

"I'm going to draw you a thank you picture," Dora announces. "I'll be back. Don't leave, Kita."

"Stay right here." Georgie points at Nikita's feet. "I'm going to make a better picture. "

"No, you won't." Dora tugs at her sister's arm.

"I will," Georgie insists as they race around the corner toward their bedroom.

I turn my attention back to Nikita. She has three brothers, but she knows that I'm only a phone call away if she ever needs anything. "What's wrong?"

"Did I say something was wrong?" she teases. "Maybe something is very right."

Our bond is almost identical to the one I share with Delia, so I playfully tap her on the shoulder. "What's very right?"

With a flourish, she dips her hand into the pocket of her jean jacket. She tugs out a chocolate bar. "I brought this for you."

I tap my stomach. "I'm trying to stay in shape."

"Do that after you open this one." She drops it in my hand. "I made it just for you."

The way she's grinning from ear to ear tells me that this isn't a run-of-the-mill candy bar.

"What the hell is going on, Nikita?"

She leans closer to plant a kiss on my cheek. "You're like a brother to me, Rome, but I promised I wouldn't say a word. My job was to give you this chocolate bar and walk away."

I look down at it before I level my gaze back on her. I'm almost afraid to ask, but I do. "Bianca?"

She mimes locking her lips and tossing the imaginary key away while she nods.

My heart skips a beat. "I need to open this."

"Kita!" Georgie calls from the end of the hallway. "Come and see what we're making for you."

Nikita steps around me. "Bianca is the sweetest person, Roman. She's perfect for you."

She's right. Bianca is perfect for me.

I tear open the wrapper, toss the chocolate bar on the foyer table, and read the note that's tucked under it.

Meet me at Bow Bridge in Central Park today at 6 PM.

I glance at the watch on my wrist. "Shit."

"I'll watch the girls," Nikita says from behind me. "You go to her. I've got things covered here."

I turn and stalk toward where she's standing with Georgie by her side. Scooping my daughter into my arms, I plant a kiss on her forehead. She giggles.

Dora runs at me full speed, so I crouch down and take her into my embrace too.

I glance up at Nikita. "Matt will be home by seven. I'll text him to relieve you."

"Daddy's going out!" Dora grabs ahold of Georgie's shoulder. "We can have pizza."

"I'll order a pepperoni pizza," Nikita chimes in.

"This is the best day ever!" Georgie bounces up and down with her brown hair flying around her shoulders.

"It is," I agree with a tremor in my voice.

Bianca wants to see me at the place I go to celebrate. This may very well be a close second when it comes to the best days of my life. The first was when the two little girls clinging tightly to me were born.

Chapter 42

Bianca

After Vivi left my apartment earlier, I ran to Wolf Candy. I met Nikita, who is not only beautiful but also incredibly thoughtful.

I explained who I was without going into too much detail. I could tell by the way she smiled at me that she knows that my feelings for Roman run deep.

She was excited when I asked if she could help me send Roman a message wrapped in a chocolate bar just as he'd done for me.

She handed me a pad of paper and a pen. When I was done, we sat at one of the tables in her candy store and had lemonade while I snacked on a new creation she's going to introduce soon.

It's a strawberry flavored marshmallow chocolate something that she says doesn't have a name yet.

Our conversation was easy and focused mostly on what a great friend, brother, and father Roman is.

She didn't tell me anything too personal but explained how supportive Roman has been to his siblings and her when she's needed him.

I'm not surprised.

He's the best man I've ever met.

As I was leaving the store, Nikita insisted that I keep my wallet in my purse. She told me that as soon as she was done getting the chocolate bar packaged up, she'd go and see Roman to deliver it to him.

That was more than I could have asked for.

I didn't think through how I would get the candy to him, so her offer was perfect.

I spent the rest of the afternoon at home getting ready for tonight.

Everything inside of me is telling me that Roman will show up at Bow Bridge.

I ascend the subway steps as fast as I can. It's just a few minutes before six. I took extra time picking out my outfit for tonight.

I decided to wear jeans, a black lace shirt and my favorite heels. I let my hair dry as I applied my makeup, so I'm sporting loose waves, waterproof mascara, and just a hint of lipstick.

I dart into Central Park headed straight for Bow Bridge.

It's a warm evening, so there are a lot of people on the path. I weave around a couple with two kids in tow and an older man walking a dog.

I wave at everybody I pass because my dad taught me that a stranger's kindness could make or break a person's day.

I know a smile from someone I've never met has brightened my mood when I've been stuck in a rut feeling sorry for myself.

I take quick steps as I make my way through the park.

My gaze darts down to my phone over and over as I watch the seconds tick away as it nears the top of the hour.

I slow when I can finally see the bridge because he's there.

Roman is standing on the bridge deck, holding a single pink daisy as he waits for me.

***

"Bianca." My name escapes him in a low growl. "Jesus, you're breathtaking. How are you more beautiful every time I see you?"

If any other man said those words to me, I'd doubt them, but I don't with Roman. He means them. I see it in his eyes.

"You look pretty great yourself," I say as I look over the dark jeans and black button-down shirt he's wearing.

It's not tucked in, and the sleeves are rolled up to his elbows. He looks comfortable, but I can sense that he's tense. The hard set of his jaw gives that away.

"This is for you." He pushes the daisy at me.

I take it, shivering as our fingers brush. "Thank you."

He steps closer to me. "Bianca, I'm so fucking sorry."

I quiet him with a press of my finger to his chin. "For what, Roman? For protecting your children? For being sure before you introduced me to them?"

His hand reaches up to grab mine. He cups it gently against his chest. "For not telling you they existed. You've had a lot thrown at you in the past twenty-four hours. First, Matthew, and then Dora and Georgie."

"Your family," I say softly. "I got to see your family."

"You met Matt." He lets out a chuckle. "In a very memorable way. I want you to meet Dora and Georgie."

Even though I'm never put a lot of thought into having children of my own, I've been excited to meet Maren's baby. That pales in comparison to how desperately I want to meet Roman's daughters. "I want that to happen."

"When?"

The question startles me enough that I take a step back. I suck in a breath and answer honestly. "As soon as you feel it's the right time."

"Tomorrow?" he says. "If that works for you, I'd like you to come over tomorrow."

"To your home?"

"The apartment I bought after Dora and Georgie's mom blew out of town." He hangs his head. "I want to explain all of that to you."

"You will." I step closer to rest my head against his chest. "If you can, I'd like you to come home with me."

He glances down and into my face. "Now?"

"Now." I nod before I tickle his chin with the daisy. "Unless you want the flower to decide for you."

"Hell no." He presses a kiss to my forehead. "I'm coming home with you. There's no place I'd rather be."

Chapter 43

Roman

I stare into Bianca's eyes, not surprised at all by the compassion I see there.

She moves closer to me. We've been sitting on the couch in her living room since we got here from Bow Bridge.

We sipped wine, and she talked about work.

I urged her to because I needed a minute to gather my thoughts. I have years of confessions to make, and I want to be sure that she's ready for it all.

"Tell me about your daughters' mother."

There it is - the first step down a path to the past. I take one final sip of wine before I place the glass down on the coffee table. "Elizabeth is her name. We met at a gallery opening. I was there because a client asked me to be. Elizabeth was looking for a new piece for her art collection."

She nods. "You hit it off?"

There's no shame in this story. I was single. Elizabeth was too, at the time. She was newly divorced and looking for someone to help her get past the pain of that. I was there, eager and willing.

"We slept together that night," I confess. "The condom broke, although neither of us thought much of it. I was clean, she assured me she was as well, and she was on birth control."

"But still…" Bianca's voice trails.

"Yes." I tilt my chin down. "We saw each other a few times in the weeks that followed. When we realized we weren't a good match, we parted ways on good terms."

I wait for her to comment, but she doesn't say a word.

"She was a couple of months along when she realized she was pregnant." I look to the floor. "We talked it through and decided for the sake of our baby that we'd give things another go."

"Babies," she corrects me.

I smile. "We didn't realize that at the time. Once we found out we were expecting twins, things became strained."

Bianca nods. "It would be a lot for anyone."

"It wasn't for me," I say honestly. "I was over the moon. I'm a twin. I know what a gift that is. I've always had Matt on my side. He's been right there from day one, so to learn that my daughters would have that too…well, it brought me to tears during the sonogram appointment."

Her hand reaches out to cover mine in my lap. "I understand."

"Elizabeth didn't." I chuckle. "For the remainder of the pregnancy we cycled between talking about marriage and custody agreements because she wanted to break up."

A frown mars Bianca's face. "That sounds so stressful at such a special time."

I toss my head back. "It was hell. We finally decided to commit to each other, but without the legal ties, so I bought the penthouse that she wanted, and we moved in. The girls arrived, and less than two months later, Elizabeth left."

Bianca shifts her legs. "Left? She moved out and got her own place?"

"She moved to Los Angeles," I explain. "She was offered a job on the west coast while she was pregnant. She turned it down, but when they circled back and asked again after the girls were born, she accepted it."

Her face falls. "She didn't consult you?"

The laugh that escapes me would have been laced with bitterness if not for the fact that I felt nothing but relief when Elizabeth left. That shifted to sadness when I realized that my daughters would never have a solid relationship with their mom.

"Elizabeth does what Elizabeth wants." I exhale. "She made an effort to see the girls a couple of times before their first birthday, but I was granted full custody shortly after that, and she's been a ghost since."

"She doesn't spend time with them?"

Shaking my head, I squeeze her hand. "No. I don't expect she ever will."

"I'm so sorry." She scoots across the leather of the couch until our thighs are touching. "I'm sorry you've had to deal with that, but my heart breaks for your kids."

Genuine concern swims in her expression as she goes on, "I imagine it hasn't always been easy for you, but from what I saw earlier today, you have two very happy little girls in your life. You must be an amazing dad."

"They make it easy."

Her eyes lock on mine. "I had no idea that I was falling for a hot single dad."

The corners of my lips curve up. "You're falling for me?"

"Hard," she says with a giggle.

"Give me a kiss, and I will be," I tease.

She takes it seriously as she leans closer, trails her tongue over her bottom lip, and kisses me deeply.

Chapter 44

Bianca

This moment in time will be etched in my heart and memory forever.

Roman dove between my legs when he stripped me as we walked into my bedroom. His clothes were on the floor just as fast, but once I had come under his tongue, he cradled me in his arms and stared into my eyes.

We must have stayed like that, entangled in each other in every way for more than thirty minutes.

We just breathed and studied each other.

For the very first time, I noticed a small mole next to Roman's left ear. He trailed his fingertip over the freckle that sits to the right of the center of my forehead.

I wanted to save his face to my memory because I fell in love with him tonight.

I may have doubted it until now, but as we shared silence and an intense connection that needed no words, I felt myself open to him.

My heart has never felt this tied to another person before.

I've never been as content with today and anticipated tomorrow as much as I do right now.

Roman's above me now, his sheathed cock slowly thrusting into me. His movements are measured and gentle. There's no rush for an orgasm. We're just savoring this – our first time making love with open hearts.

"You're so incredible," he says in a low tone.

"Roman," I manage his name but nothing else.

He moves to rest his lips against mine as he takes me closer to the edge with each stroke. "You feel so good. This is so good."

He slows the pace to an almost unbearable movement. It leaves me wanting and eager for my release.

"Roman," I protest on a moan. "Don't stop."

His eyes find mine. He stares into me, past the pain of every relationship I've ever had and every doubt that has flooded me about what my future holds. "I can't stop. We were made for each other."

With a press of his lips to mine for a lush kiss, he ups his pace. He fucks me with his eyes locked on mine until I come no more than a minute before he does.

***

I turn over to watch him from behind as he answers his phone.

It's near midnight. We've been in bed for hours, talking and touching. Kissing and fucking.

I got up briefly to make us a salad, but Roman had me over his shoulder before I could finish. He carried me back to bed, tossed me into the middle of it, and touched me until I came again.

I'm sore and satisfied in a way that feels perfect.

"How much pizza did she eat?" he asks someone. "Dora can't handle all that cheese."

He turns to face me. A smile brightens his face immediately.

"You're a goddamn doctor." He laughs. "I know you're a vet, but c'mon you must have a cure for a stomachache."

His hand trails down his nude body to his stomach. My gaze follows it but dips below to see his cock half-erect.

"Dad hugs are the cure," he says quietly. "I'm on my way."

I smile as he ends the call and lowers his phone. "You're right. Dad hugs are the best hugs."

He stalks toward the bed. "I hate to leave you like this, but I need to go."

I swing my bare legs over the side of the mattress. "I know."

Before I can stand, he's on his knees on the floor in front of the bed. He wraps his arms around my legs until his hands rest on the top of my ass. "I've been looking for you my entire life."

I rake my hands through his hair, pushing it back from his forehead. "I can say the same to you."

"A very wise man once told me that with an open heart anything is possible." He moves to kiss my shoulder. "He was right."

"My dad used to say that," I whisper.

"Smart man." He pulls back to look into my face. "Tonight meant everything to me. I have a feeling tomorrow will be just as special."

"You'll text me the time and place?"

"I will."

I suck in a breath. "Should I bring anything?"

"No. I just want you there." He smiles in the softest way. "I want you there to meet my two little girls."

Chapter 45

Roman

Trying to calm the girls down isn't happening. Georgie is bouncing up and down on the small trampoline Matt dragged in here a few weeks ago. Dora is running circles around her with the makeshift pink bandage wrapped around her head again.

I'm all about making a great first impression, but I want these two to be their authentic selves.

They're two loving, inquisitive, and very energetic six-year-olds.

"When will Bianca be here?" Georgie says as she drops into another bounce.

Dora's finger juts out to point at her as she rounds the corner of the living room in a sprint. "You said her name right this time."

Georgie struggled with the pronunciation of Bianca's name. She put an extra '*n*' sound before the '*anca*.' It came out sounding like Binanca. It was fucking adorable.

I was all for it, but Dora wasn't having it.

She stood in front of the trampoline while Georgie recited Bianca's name over and over again on each bounce.

Dora finally gave up on the twenty-second try.

"I know I did," Georgie yells in her outside voice. "It's Binanca Marks."

That stops Dora in her tracks. "Oh brother, not again."

I hold back a grin as I tidy the dining room table. It's a futile move since all the coloring books, crayons, and puzzles will be dumped back there within the hour.

Every night, we gather there for an hour to go over the day's schoolwork, do a craft, or work on a puzzle altogether. Matt, or one of my other siblings, often joins in.

My mom does too, when she's in town.

She's settled in Maine for the spring and summer and comes back to New York each winter. I've often heard her comment that one day she'll spend all of her time in this city with her grandchildren.

I don't know if that day will come.

She's enjoying her retirement. She worked hard to support the four of us after our dad walked out.

"Dora, it's all good," I call out to her just as she's about to get her sister to repeat Bianca's name again. "Are you going to change your clothes before Bianca gets here?"

Her hands drift out to her sides. "Why would I?"

I should point out that she's wearing two different colored knee-high socks. One is purple, the other pink. Neither matches the bright green neon shorts she's wearing or the canary yellow T-shirt.

Georgie chose a pink dress.

The days of them wearing matching clothing are in the rearview mirror.

They are as distinctly different as two six-year-olds can be.

A knock at the door sends both girls rushing toward it. This is it. This is the moment when my girls meet the woman I love.

I'm on their heels, but I'm too slow.

Georgie swings open the door and launches herself into Bianca's arms. "Hi, Binanca."

Bianca's eyes lock on mine as she cradles my daughter against her. "Hi."

"I'm Dora." Dora tugs on the bottom of the white sweater Bianca's wearing. "That's Georgie."

"It's nice to meet you both," Bianca says softly.

"We're happy to know you." Dora drags the end of the ribbon wrapped around her head to the side. "Daddy likes you a lot. He said you're his girlfriend."

Both of my girls erupt into high-pitched laughter.

I curve a finger to lure Bianca into my home. "Please, come in. Join us."

She motions to a paper shopping bag on the floor. "I brought a few gifts. I hope that's alright."

"We love gifts." Georgie squirms free from Bianca's arms and lands on her feet on the floor.

Dora grabs one twine handle of the bag. Georgie takes control of the other. They carry it together into the foyer as I reach out a hand to Bianca.

She takes it happily. "They're amazing little girls, Roman."

"Thank you for the coloring books!" Georgie chirps from behind me.

"Thank you more for the new crayons!" Dora joins in.

I tug Bianca closer. "Get ready to have the time of your life."

***

"You color inside the lines." Georgie runs a fingertip over the picture of a tiger that Bianca has spent the last thirty minutes working on. "You're good."

Bianca offers my daughter a soft smile. "I'm good? Look at your creation."

Georgie's gaze dips to the picture of an elephant on the table in front of her. As usual, it's a combination of mixed shades of pink and red. She skims a hand over it. "Do you like it, Binanca?"

"She loves it." Dora spreads her arms wide. "This much."

Bianca nods in agreement. "I like both of your pictures that much."

Dora smiles. "This isn't my best work, but I think I did good."

"It's perfect," Bianca comments as she studies the picture of a dog. "I really like the way you colored his nose blue."

"If I had a dog, I'd name him Blue," she announces with a glare in my direction. "Daddy says no pets until we're older."

I shrug. "When you two can help take care of a dog, we'll get one."

"I can take care of one." Georgie's hand pops into the air. "I want to name it Orange."

"Why?" Dora asks in exasperation. "That makes no sense."

"I had a dog named February when I was little." Bianca laughs. "I think a dog's name can be whatever you want it to be."

"February?" I question with a perk of my brow. "What's the story behind that?"

"My sister named him that." She sighs. "I went along with it because I thought it was different."

"Oh, it is." Dora nods. "I don't know any dogs named February."

"Maybe Uncle Matty does!" Georgie exclaims as she slides to her feet. "Let's call and ask him."

"Uncle Matt is enjoying a day off." I gather Georgie into my arms. "We'll call him before bed tonight."

She cups both of her hands around my cheeks. "Deal."

Dora darts to her feet to wrap her arms around my neck. "Double deal."

Both of my daughters turn to look at Bianca.

"Make it a triple deal, Binanca." Georgie summons her with a curl of her fingers. "Hug us."

Bianca is on her feet in an instant. When she rounds me to wrap her arms around my daughters and me, I feel something I've never felt before.

Complete.

Chapter 46

Bianca

"You got another mystery package." Paige stands at the entrance to my office waving a large blue envelope in the air. "It's too big to be an engagement ring and too flat to be anything but a document."

I laugh. "Your dress matches that envelope."

She gazes down at the robin blue egg sheath dress she's wearing. "I have excellent taste, as does Dora George. No, I think it says Dora Georgie. Is that a new contractor?"

She takes a step toward the corner window in my office. Holding the envelope near the sunlight streaming in, she studies it.

"Are you trying to see what's inside of there? I'm sitting right here, Paige."

Laughing, she drops the envelope on the corner of my desk. "The handwriting is…well, it's…I don't want to say childish, but maybe elementary is a better word. Don't tell Dora George I said that."

"I won't," I assure her with a grin.

"You seem happier than I've ever seen you, Bianca."

"I am," I answer without hesitation. "I'm really happy."

A smile blooms on her lips. "Does it have to do with the gorgeous suit who stopped by a few weeks ago?"

I see no reason to avoid this discussion since Vivi already knows that I'm crazy in love with Roman. "Everything to do with him."

"Good."

I glance at the envelope she dropped on my desk. "I should open this."

"In private," she adds. "I'll shut the door on my way out."

"Thank you."

She hesitates briefly. "It's inspiring to see your happily-ever-after playing out. It gives me hope that somewhere in this vast city, there's a great guy just waiting for me too."

"There is," I say with conviction.

"I believe you." Her face brightens. "One day I'll find him."

I have no doubt she will.

As soon as she clicks my office door shut, I rip into the envelope that Georgie and Dora addressed.

It's obvious that the pencil-written letters on the front of the envelope came from two different hands. One has a more precise grasp on the shape of the letters. The other has a more carefree approach.

I haven't spent a lot of time with Georgie and Dora, but I watched Georgie take her time writing her name on the picture she colored two nights ago. Dora grabbed a blue crayon and scribbled her name with a flourish of her hand.

I peek inside the envelope to find a handwritten letter and two colored pictures.

One of the pictures looks like it's a red and blue polka-dot daisy with missing petals. The other is a striped daisy with yellow leaves.

Georgie signed the first. Dora's signature covers the stem of the daisy on the second.

Their dad wrote the note.

Your company is requested for dinner at our home.

Tomorrow. 6PM.

Bring your smile.

Under Roman's handwriting are scribbles that I take to be XO written over and over with different colored crayons.

Tears fill my eyes as I hold the note and the drawings close to my chest.

I glance at the picture of my dad on my desk as a lone tear falls down my cheek. "I found him, dad. I found the man who will take care of my heart forever."

Months before my father died, we were picking daisies in the field across from our apartment building when I started plucking the petals and reciting, "he loves me, he loves me not," over and over.

My dad stopped me with a hand on my shoulder. He crouched down with his shoes sinking into the soft soil, and he told me when I was all grown-up, I'd find a man who would take care of my heart forever.

He smiled as he said that once that happened, I wouldn't need a daisy to tell me he loved me. I'd know.

"He loves me too," I say to the picture of my dad. "Roman loves me too."

***

"Are those cupcakes?" Dora screams as soon as she spots the white box in my hands. "Did you bring cupcakes for Georgie and me?"

I look toward where Roman is standing in the middle of the living room. He has Georgie in his arms. I can tell she's been crying. Her tear-soaked cheeks are as red as her eyes.

"Is everything all right?" I tentatively ask as I step into the foyer, shutting the door behind me.

"I…I fell…" Georgie sobs. "I wanted to answer the door when you knocked, but I fell."

"Hard," Dora chimes in.

Roman kisses his daughter on the cheek before she slides to the ground. Her small hands tug at the hem of her blue and white patterned dress.

"Daddy brings us cupcakes on Saturdays," Dora says. "Today isn't Saturday."

I nod. "It's not, but your dad told me it would be okay if you had one after dinner."

"One each?" Georgie asks quietly. "I get one, and Dora gets one, Binanca?"

My heart feels like it swells inside my chest whenever I hear her say my name. "One each. I also brought some stickers."

"Stickers!" Dora twirls in a circle, sending her dark hair flowing around her head. "I love stickers."

I tug the package of stickers I found at a shop near my office out of the purse slung over my shoulder. "I thought you could share."

Dora takes them from my hand. "Thank you."

"Thank you," Georgie echoes from where she's standing. "I like your shirt, Binanca."

I glance down at the yellow T-shirt I'm wearing and the jeans I put on as soon as I got home from work.

"It matches my skirt," Dora says, pointing at one of the brightly colored lemons on the green skirt she's wearing.

She's topped her outfit with a heavy blue sweater, and the addition of red tights makes the entire look adorable.

Dora rips open the package of stickers, yanks one of a puppy free, and slaps it in the middle of her forehead.

Georgie giggles before she races over, tugs a sticker of a rainbow into her palm. It ends up on her cheek.

"How do we look?" she asks with outstretched arms.

"Beautiful," I whisper. "You're both so beautiful."

Chapter 47

Roman

I glance over to see Bianca cutting a tomato. This feels good. It feels so damn good to have her here.

"How are you doing?" I ask softly. "Are you good?"

The smile on her face answers the question before she does. "I'm so good, Roman."

I season the salmon steaks that I bought on my way home from work. "The girls adore you."

Resting the knife down on the cutting board, Bianca turns toward me. "I feel the same way about them. I haven't been around many kids, but they're special. They seem special to me."

I glance down because I'm overcome with emotion.

When she first sat down next to me at Rolly's, I wanted her. I wanted to kiss her and fuck her. I wanted to experience that with her, but it's different now.

I still want that. Jesus, do I want that.

I also want this. It's a weekday dinner that we cook together side-by-side while my girls play in the main room. I want her here for our bedtime story and breakfast. Hell, I want her here all the time.

Closing the distance between us with a few heavy steps, I lower my voice. "This feels right."

She gazes into my eyes. "It does to me too."

The words I've been longing to say to her sit on my lips. I want Bianca to understand the depth of my feelings. I need her to know that I'd move heaven and earth to make her happy. I love her.

Instead of saying a thing, I lean forward and kiss her softly on the mouth.

"Daddy!" Dora screeches from a few feet away. "Daddy loves Bianca. He's kissing her."

Bianca's gaze darts behind her, but I keep mine on the woman I love.

Georgie comes racing in. "I missed the kiss."

Bianca turns back to me to press her lips against my cheek. "There's another kiss."

Georgie claps her hands in the air. "I saw it. They are in love."

Bianca smiles softly. "We should finish getting dinner ready."

I nod. "Let's do that."

Dora and Georgie disappear around the corner again.

"How do you feel about seeing me again tomorrow, Bianca?"

Her gaze flits over my face. "I'd love that."

"I'll bring something to your place for dinner," I offer. "Around eight?"

Her lips land on mine for a deep kiss. "That's perfect. I can't wait."

I can't either because tomorrow I tell this remarkable woman how I feel about her. I want Bianca Marks to know that I love her.

***

"Do you have a job?" Georgie threads her fork through the flesh of the salmon on her plate before she shoves a piece into her mouth.

Bianca nods. "I do. I'm a senior project manager at a company that builds really tall buildings."

"No way." Dora darts to her feet. "That's what I want to be."

"No." Georgie follows her sister's lead and slides off her chair to stand. "You want to be a vet like Uncle Matty. I want to be a lawyer."

"I don't want to be a vet," Dora announces with a brisk shake of her head. "I changed my mind."

Georgie's hands drop to her hips. "You can't."

"I can so," Dora disagrees. "Daddy said I could be whatever I want to be, so I want to be what Bianca is."

"She already has that job," Georgie points out. "So you can't have it."

"She's going to retire soon like grandma did."

Bianca lets out a laugh. "I have a few years before I retire, and besides, one day, I hope I'll own a real estate development company of my own."

I turn to look at her. "Really?"

"Really," she repeats, her tone brimming with confidence. "I have so many connections in this city. I believe in ten years, I can branch out on my own."

I'm so fucking proud of her. I'm so goddamn happy that she's sharing this in front of my daughters. I want them to reach for the stars too, until they have them in their grasp.

"You'll do it," I say assuredly. "You're going to do it, Bianca."

"You will," Georgie chimes in.

Dora rushes around the table until she's standing next to Bianca. "I know you'll do it. Daddy says a person can do anything with hard work."

"And the right attic dudes," Georgie adds.

Bianca drops her chin to hide the grin on her face.

"Attitude," Dora corrects her sister.

I soak it all in. This is life. This is what I want every fucking night of my life.

"Let's finish dinner so we can have a cupcake," Bianca suggests. "I brought a lot of different flavors."

"First pick!" Georgie calls as she takes a seat in her chair.

"Seconds," Dora says as she settles back behind the table.

"Third," Bianca whispers.

I turn to look at her to find tears welling in her eyes.

"This is the best dinner I've had in a very long time," she confesses softly.

I take her hand in mine. "Me too."

Chapter 48

Bianca

I watch in awe as Roman gathers his daughters into his arms after they get their pajamas on.

His gentle hand runs over the back of Georgie's head. "You're tired."

"So tired, daddy," she agrees with a nod of her chin. "But you'll tell us a story, right?"

Roman looks to where I'm standing in the doorway of his daughters' bedroom.

As soon as I glanced into this room, I had an uncontrollable smile on my lips. Half of the walls in the room are soft pink. The other half is a mix of many different colors. It appears as if someone haphazardly threw pink, blue, orange, yellow, and purple paint against those walls.

I knew before Georgie jumped onto her bed which side of the room belonged to her. It's the pink side, with the books aligned in a row on a shelf and her slippers set out next to the bed. A few stuffed animals are sitting next to her pillow.

Dora's side of the room is a reflection of who she is. It's messy but filled with charm. There are a few pictures hung on the wall near her bed. They are hand-drawn. Each is signed at the bottom with her first name. Stuffed animals are tucked under the blanket, and a flashlight sits on the nightstand within her reach.

"This is for emergencies," she told me when she saw me looking at it.

My dad put one on a desk in the room I shared with Vivi when we were kids. He told us to use it if the power ever went out in the middle of the night. My sister responded that we'd be asleep and wouldn't notice.

I'll never forget how hard my dad laughed at that.

"Maybe Bianca can tell a story?" Roman questions with a perk of his brows. "I bet she has a lot of great stories."

The girls jump onto their respective beds.

"Tell us a story!" Georgie yells.

Dora repeats her words in an even louder tone.

I grab the back of one of the two small wooden chairs sitting next to a table in the corner. I drag it across the carpet and take a seat.

Roman settles next to Georgie. Dora bounces from her bed to the floor and then onto Georgie's bed in one seamless move.

"What should the story be about?" I ask, wondering what I've gotten myself into.

"Do you have a brother?" Georgie asks as she cuddles in next to Roman.

"I do," I answer quietly. "Gray."

"A crayon is your brother?" Dora giggles.

Roman lets out a chuckle. "Bianca's brother isn't a crayon."

"His name is Grayson," I clarify with a smile. "Grayson Marks."

"Tell us your dad's name," Georgie hesitates. "Please, Binanca. What's his name?"

"Thurston," Roman says quickly.

"George." My voice overlaps his.

His gaze darts to my face. "What? Thurston Marks is your father. That's what you told Clarice."

"Stepfather," I say quietly. "My father…my dad... well, his name was George."

"Like me?" Georgie bounces to her feet. "Your dad was named Georgie like me?"

Roman leans forward. "You said *was*, Bianca."

I nod. "He's not here anymore."

"He died?" he asks.

Georgie's hand darts to her mouth as Dora lets out a gasp.

I shake my head. "It was a very long time ago. I was lucky that I got to have him as a dad for eleven years. Now, I have a dad named Thurston."

"Two dads." Georgie smiles. "That is lucky."

"Your father died when you were eleven?" Roman's gaze searches my face. "How?"

"It was very sudden. He had a heart attack," I whisper. "He was in Kentucky on business when it happened. Should we talk about this later?"

"His heart was sick?" Dora's tone is soft. "Our great-grandma got sick. She died before we were born."

"I'm so sorry," I say to both girls. "I'm sure she was very special."

"Daddy said she was the best grandma."

I look at Roman, but I can't read his expression, so I change the subject. "I think I should tell you a story about my sister, Viviana."

"Vivranna." Georgie stumbles over her name.

"Vivi," I whisper. "I call her that, or sometimes I call her V."

"V?" Dora giggles. "I like that. I could be D."

"I could be G," Georgie joins in.

"I'm B." I raise my hand in the air. "Vivi calls me that. We're B and V."

"B and V," Roman repeats with a tremor in his tone. "Wait. Your surname. Thurston adopted you?"

Nodding, I turn my full attention to him. "I was born a Cuthbert. I was adopted when I was twelve by Thurston after he married my mom."

All the color drains from his face. "I had no idea."

"Are you all right?" I ask quietly.

"Sometimes salmon gives daddy a tummy ache." Georgie grasps her stomach. "It does that to me too."

"Me three." Dora throws herself back onto the bed. "Buggy too. I think we need to call Uncle Matty."

I hold back a smile. "I feel fine."

There's no hint of amusement in Roman's expression when he locks eyes with me. "I think we need to call it a night. It's way past the girls' bedtime."

"Daddy, no," Dora protests. "Bianca was going to tell us a story about V."

"V and B," he says softly. "It's late. You both need to get into bed."

Georgie yawns. "I'm sleepy."

I wait for Roman to tuck the girls in, but no one moves, so I do.

I slide to my feet. "I'll take off."

Roman follows my lead. The girls both hop up too.

I step aside as the three of them hold hands, and make their way out of the bedroom, down the hallway and to the foyer. I follow in silence behind them.

My stomach knots as I scoop up my purse from the dining room table.

Something shifted hard in that bedroom, and I have no idea what caused it.

"Thanks for coming, Bianca," Roman says in the same tone he used when he spoke to Clarice Blanchard on the sidewalk.

It's devoid of affection or the reassuring comfort that is always there when he says my name.

"I'm glad I did," I reply, trying to hide the emotion in my voice.

"Bye B," Georgie rushes at me.

I run a hand over her head as she wraps her arms around my legs.

Dora joins in with a whispered, "I'll miss you."

I hug them close to me before they both step away.

"Come back soon." Georgie rubs at her eyes.

I glance at Roman, but he's staring at his children.

"Goodnight," I say to the girls.

"Goodnight," they respond in their sweet voices.

Roman finally raises his head to look directly at me. "Goodnight, Bianca."

I stare at him. I don't see the same openness that was there when I arrived. His gaze is hollow and empty. Sadness has settled over him.

"Goodnight," I say in return as I walk out of his apartment, wondering if I'll ever be invited back.

Chapter 49

Bianca

Roman: ***I have an unexpected meeting tonight. I'm sorry, but I can't make it.***

I must have read Roman's text message ten times in the two days since he sent it. It took me hours to reply because I had no idea what to say.

Part of me wanted to respond with a question about what the hell happened at his apartment the other night.

Another part of me thought it might be best to firm up a new night for our date.

I didn't go with either.

My response to his text was swift and short.

Bianca: OK.

I haven't heard anything from him since. That makes it almost seventy-two hours since I last saw him.

I hope with everything that I am that it wasn't the last time I'll ever see him.

I glance up when I hear the door to my apartment open.

I expected Vivi to show up tonight with food. My sister can read between the lines whenever we're talking or texting.

We've done a lot of both the last few days.

I kept putting her off by telling her I'd see her next week, but when I broke down in tears during a call this afternoon, she whispered that she'd bring dinner to my apartment as soon as she was done with work.

I skim a hand over the sweatpants I'm wearing. I was in them as soon as I got home from the office. I paired them with a New York Mets shirt I picked up last week.

I wanted to be wearing it and panties when Roman arrived one night.

I may never get that chance now.

"What's wrong?" Vivi's voice trembles as she sets down a large bag and her purse on the foyer table. "I'm worried, B."

I run at her with my arms outstretched. She's a bit taller than me, but we've always fit together perfectly.

She clings to me as I work my way through a sob. "I don't know."

Her hand pats the center of my back. "You don't know what's wrong?"

I let out a hiccup as I pull back from our embrace. "I don't know."

A smile blooms on her lips. "We'll figure it out together. Have you eaten today?"

I shake my head. "I tried to eat lunch, but I couldn't."

"I brought soup." She points at the bag. "And some crackers. There is a piece of cherry pie in there for you too."

"We'll share," I whisper as I look into her eyes.

"Absolutely. I'm going to dish this up. Why don't you sit down at the table and relax?"

I nod as I watch her grab the bag and breeze past me on her way to my kitchen.

I don't know when my little sister grew up, but I'm glad she did. She's the only person I want with me now.

***

Vivi taps her spoon against the empty bowl in front of her. "Do you want dessert now?"

She's kept my mind occupied through dinner. She talked about what she did at work today. She booked two weddings, an engagement party, and what sounds like a very elaborate sweet sixteen birthday party.

I managed a smile when she bounced out of her chair to show me a dance move that one of the people she works with taught her doing lunch.

Vivi is many things, but she's not a good dancer. I've always told her that she missed out on the rhythm gene I inherited from our mom.

"It's Roman," I blurt out. "Something happened with him."

She bites the corner of her bottom lip. "He didn't cheat on you, did he? If he did, I'll find him. I will give him a piece of my mind just like I did with Kieran."

"You talked to Kieran?"

The laugh that escapes her is fleeting. "Not exactly. I yelled at him on the sidewalk in front of his apartment building."

"What?"

"He deserved it." She places the spoon down on the table. "He hurt you. I couldn't let him get away with that."

I thought Thurston would be the one to confront Kieran. I had no idea Vivi would do it.

"That wasn't necessary, V."

"Oh yes, it was." She chuckles. "It made me feel better. I hope he thinks twice before he cheats on another woman."

I hope so too. Even though I wasn't devastated by Kieran's actions, I know that level of betrayal can break some people. I wouldn't wish that on anyone.

"Roman didn't cheat," I say softly. "He closed up when I was at his apartment."

She rests her elbows on the table. "Closed up? How?"

I finally let out my first big exhale in days. "I was telling him and the girls about our family. Grayson, Thurston, you, dad…and he just shut down."

"Why?"

That's the million dollar question I don't have an answer to.

I shrug. "I'm not sure."

"Ask him."

"How?"

She points to where my phone is on the coffee table. "Call him and ask him what the hell is going on, Bianca."

"Just like that," I tease.

"You're reading between the lines." She skims a hand over her forehead. "Maybe something you said upset him. Did his dad die? That could have been a trigger for him."

"I'm not sure."

"You won't be sure until you ask him." Her gaze darts to my phone again. "Get a good night's sleep and then call him tomorrow. Tell him you need to see him."

"What if he doesn't answer?" I ask.

"Leave a message." Her hand reaches for mine. "You've never been in love, so I get this is new, but you can't twist yourself up because of this. It could be a misunderstanding, but you can't know that until you reach out to him."

"How are you so smart?" I narrow my eyes. "You've never been in love either."

"I will be one day," she says confidently. "When I fall in love, I'll hold tight to him. You're going to do that with Roman too."

"I am."

"Do you want to skip the pie and go there?" she stresses the last word. "It might help."

There.

It's a weathered wooden bench that sits in the alley near a bodega on the Lower East Side. Our dad would take us to the bodega, buy us each a popsicle, and the three of us would sit on the bench and talk.

The bench is still there, so whenever Vivi or I need an escape, we go to the bodega together, buy two grape flavored popsicles, and then we sit on the bench.

Sometimes we talk, other times we share silence, but we do it side-by-side.

I nod. "I'll grab a sweater."

"Ditch that shirt while you're at it." She laughs. "Daddy would have loved it, but the New York Yankees are our team, remember?"

I smooth a hand down the front of the shirt. "I remember. The shirt stays on. Maybe we need to consider being fans of both teams."

She purses her lips. "You might have something there. Double the fun and all."

I laugh for the first time in days. "Double the fun."

Chapter 50

Roman

Some secrets can stay buried for eternity. Others can't.

The one that Angela Marks thought she'd take to her grave came back to haunt her in the form of a phone call from me.

That happened two days ago after Chad tracked down her cell number for me from a woman named Shirlene. I didn't ask for that story because it didn't matter. I had Bianca's mother's number. That's all I wanted.

When I introduced myself as the man who is madly in love with her daughter, she was surprised.

When I explained my connection to her past, she hung up on me.

Then she set her husband, Thurston Marks, to my office.

The man could hold the attention of all of Manhattan just by using his charm and wit. Neither worked on me.

I'm a parent, so I understand, in an abstract way, that Angela was doing what she thought was best at the worst time in her life, but I can't keep her secret hidden.

I promised Bianca I'd never lie to her, and I have every intention of keeping that promise.

I sprint up the sidewalk toward her office building.

I thought about calling, but I have no idea if her mother or Thurston has had a chance to talk to her.

Both asked me, in very different ways, if I'd consider forgetting what I know.

Angela called me early this morning, begging me to leave her daughter alone.

I told her that I intended to marry Bianca one day, so leaving her alone was never going to happen.

Thurston took a more hands-on approach.

He showed up at my office an hour ago with a check in his hand. There were many zeroes, and my name written in blue ink. He wanted me to ghost the woman I adore in exchange for cold hard cash.

I tore up the check and laughed in his face.

I look straight ahead as I approach the lobby doors of the tower that houses the office of Packton Properties.

I spot her as she approaches the building from the opposite direction.

My beautiful Bianca is dressed in pink. Her hair is blowing in the wind. She's hurrying along on heels that should be illegal to walk in. I don't know how the hell she handles the height, but I'm not complaining.

She's breathtaking.

"Bianca," I call out to her.

Her steps slow as she searches around her. When her gaze lands on me, a smile shoots over her lips.

My world feels centered for the first time in days.

I rush toward her, sprinting around the countless people crowding this sidewalk. It's late afternoon in Manhattan. Everyone is in a goddamn hurry to get somewhere.

I know I am.

The closer I can get to the woman I love, the better I feel.

"Roman." She picks up her pace as I near her.

She's in my arms the instant I'm in front of her. I dip her, kiss her and hold her close to me until I whisper the three words I've been longing to say to her. "I love you."

Her gaze searches my face, and with a cup of her soft hand over my cheek, she says them back. "I love you, Roman. I really love you."

***

We held hands as we made our way to her apartment on the subway.

The suggestion was hers after I told her that we needed to talk. We did a pit stop at her office so she could check in with John, and then we took off.

We're at her apartment now.

I opened a bottle of white wine, poured her a glass, and then polished off one before I refilled my glass.

Even though I'm dreading the conversation we're about to have, I know I can't move forward with our relationship until I do.

This isn't a burden I'm carrying. It's a gift. A twisted, fucked up gift that I need to hand over to Bianca.

She kicks off her shoes and settles on her couch. "Sit with me?"

I'm there before she can get another breath in.

Sipping her wine, she studies my face. "Something happened the other night when I was at your place."

"Yes," I answer clearly. "Something did happen. I'm sorry for the way I handled it."

"Did your father die too, Roman?"

I shake that off with a shrug. "I'm not sure. He left when I was a kid. I've never heard from him."

Concern knits her brow. "Your father did to you what Elizabeth did to your girls?"

"He hung around for a few years after we were born, but he eventually realized he couldn't cut it."

"I'm sorry." Her hand reaches for mine. "I had no idea. When I talked about my dad dying, that must have brought up a lot of feelings for you."

I could let her make that assumption, but I won't because it's not based on fact.

I rest my wineglass on the coffee table and turn until I'm fully facing her. "When you spoke about your dad, it did bring up a lot of feelings for me."

Tears well in the corners of her eyes. "I didn't mean to be insensitive."

I swipe my finger over her cheek to catch a tear, just as I feel my emotions thundering to the surface. "You weren't, Bianca. Not at all."

She stares at me. "You felt something when I talked about him. I saw the sadness then, and I see it now."

I swallow past the lump in my throat. It's been there since she mentioned her father's name. George Cuthbert.

I suck in a deep breath and squeeze her hand in mine. "I knew your dad, Bianca."

"What?" she half-laughs. "Are you serious? He sold medical equipment. How would you have known him? You were only…"

"Sixteen when he died," I finish her sentence.

"Right." She nods. "Did your mom know him? Does she remember him?"

I drop my voice to a soft tone. "She didn't know him."

"I'm lost." She lets out a nervous laugh. "Where did you meet him?"

I bring her hand to my chest and hold it there. "At the hospital. I met him there. I visited him often, and I was holding his hand when he took his last breath."

Chapter 51

Bianca

I stare at Roman's lips. "What?"

He tilts my chin up with his fingertip, trying to draw my gaze to his. I let him. When our eyes lock, I ask him the question again. "What did you say?"

His bottom lip trembles slightly. "I met your dad when my grandmother was in Lennox Hill Hospital. He was a patient on the same ward. After she passed, I went back to see him often, and the day he died, I was there with him."

I look down at my lap. "No. You're wrong."

"I'm not."

I tug my hand free of his. "My dad died in Kentucky. He went to a medical conference there. Someone found him in his hotel room, but it was too late."

"Your father died in Manhattan on a rainy Tuesday afternoon at four-thirty," he says softly. "It was peaceful. He was comfortable. He slipped away thinking about you and your sister."

"That's another George Cuthbert." I shake my head. "My dad couldn't have died at Lennox Hill. He wasn't even in New York."

"He was in the hospital on and off for months."

"No." I move to stand. "That's not right."

"Your father had glioblastoma, Bianca."

"That's brain cancer." I drop my hands to my stomach when I feel it roll inside of me. "He didn't have that. My mom had cancer. She had ovarian cancer when I was eight."

"They wanted to protect you."

"Who?" I bark out. "My mom?"

He nods as he pushes to his feet. "Your dad too. He told me you and V had watched your mom suffer. He didn't want you to go through that again so soon. He said you were too young for that much pain."

I reach for him because I feel like I'm about to faint. "You talked to him?"

"For hours," he admits. "I didn't have a dad. He seemed like a great one, so we talked about a lot of things."

I cry out. "Tell me."

He takes me in his arms, gathering me close to him until my head is resting against his chest. "He told me he had two beautiful daughters. B and V. That's what he called you."

"He always called us that," I sob. "Always."

"George was proud of both of you." He pauses. "He told me you were an ace at math, and V was better at science."

I manage a small smile. "He was right."

"He told me about your family vacations and the Friday night pizza dinners," he goes on, "I know about the popsicle place."

"The popsicle place," I repeat. "Vivi and I went there last night."

"He told me he wanted to play professional baseball, but he didn't have the coordination."

I nod. "He always said he was clumsy."

"He loved the Mets."

I move back to glance at his face. "You love the Mets."

"Because of him."

I stare into his eyes. "What else?"

His hands reach to cup my cheeks. "When he was slipping away, he told me he loved his girls."

"Us." A rush of tears spills from my eyes. "Me and Vivi."

"I loved him," he admits as he chokes back a sob. "I met him when my grandmother was dying. I kept going back because he became my friend. He was the father figure I didn't have."

"He must have loved you too."

He drags a hand over his forehead. "He was the most important man in my life, even though I didn't know him very long."

"I can't believe you knew him," I whisper. "You knew my dad."

"I wish he was still here." He exhales. "I've wished that for a long time."

"Me too, " I admit. "I wish he could see us now."

He presses a soft kiss to my mouth. "Bianca, there's more."

I cling to the lapels of his suit jacket, not sure if my body and heart can withstand more. "What is it?"

"When the twins were born, Elizabeth hadn't considered names, so I made that decision."

I study his face. "Are you saying?"

He nods. "Dora is named after my grandmother. I named my Georgie in honor of your dad."

***

I cradle Roman's phone in my hands as I stare at a picture of his daughters.

"You named your daughter after my dad."

I feel him sit next to me. "He taught me a lot, Bianca. I wouldn't be the man I am today if it weren't for him."

I drag my gaze up to his face. "My mom must have known."

He answers first with a nod, and then he sighs. "I've spoken to your mom. I called her to ask her why you thought your father had died in another state."

My eyes widen as I feel a stab of pain rush through me. "You spoke to her?"

He scoops one of my hands into his. "I wanted her to know that I love you and that I was going to be honest with you regarding my history with your dad."

"You told her that you love me?"

"Yes," he answers succinctly. "I told her I'd do anything for you, and that includes telling you the truth."

I think that through as I study his face. "Why did this happen? Why wasn't I given a chance to see him? I would have been at that hospital every day."

He nods. "Your dad told me that you and V had watched your mother suffer after her surgery and through three rounds of chemo. They wanted to protect you from that."

"They stole my chance to say goodbye," I whisper. "I could have said goodbye to him."

"I know it's not the same, but I said goodbye to him." He tears up again. "I held his hand and told him I loved him before he closed his eyes and slipped away."

I reach a hand to cup his cheek. "Was anyone with you? Your mother? Matt?"

"No," he says, shaking his head. "I always went to the hospital alone. My mom was working. Matt would watch over Callum and Delia after school and on the weekends."

It feels surreal, but there's one thing I need to say, so I do. "Thank you for being there for him."

"It felt right." He exhales audibly. "After he died, I promised myself that I'd go back and see if anyone else needed a friend to visit with them."

"Back to the hospital?"

"It was a year or so later before I could do it, but I did." He smiles. "I've been going ever since. Mostly on Tuesday afternoons."

"We met on a Tuesday afternoon," I point out. "Had you been there before we…"

He cups my hand close to his lips to place a soft kiss on my palm. "I had just left the hospital before I headed to Rolly's. That's my usual routine."

"Really?"

"George told me that if he were granted a miracle, he'd take me to Rolly's Pub on my twenty-first birthday for a beer."

I tear up again.

"Matt and I go there every year on our birthday. We order beers and toast George."

I nod, not finding any words.

"Fate brought you to me the day we met, Bianca," he says quietly. "I think George had a hand in it too."

I move closer to him. "I think so too."

Roman stares into my eyes. "I love you. I think I fell in love with you that day."

"I love you too," I say through a veil of tears. "We were destined to be."

"You're damn right we were," he growls before he takes my mouth in a kiss.

Chapter 52

Bianca

"Mom?"

I know the instant that my mom turns to face me that her heart has broken. She looks just as she did the morning she told Vivi and me that our dad had died.

It was a rainy Wednesday. I was late getting ready for school when she appeared in the doorway to our bedroom with reddened eyes and shaking hands.

She sat us down on my bed and explained with a tremor in her voice that our dad would never come home.

His funeral service was just a few days later.

Vivi doesn't remember any of it. I recall fleeting images of a dark wood casket, pink flowers, and a hymn that my mom sang along to.

Not many people were gathered at the cemetery when he was lowered into the ground. I was given a flower to place in his grave, but I wanted him to remember me always, so I threw a picture that I had drawn on top of his casket.

It was of the four of us on a sunny afternoon with blue sky on the horizon.

I glance down at the sight of his grave now with the perfectly cut grass and the headstone that my mom had placed here a year after his death.

It was right before she married Thurston.

"Bianca." My name escapes her in a whisper.

I hold out my arms to her because I need her to know that I understand. "I'm sorry for everything you've been through, Mom."

She rushes across the grass with her heels digging into the ground. "I'm sorry, baby."

Baby.

She hasn't called me that since he passed away. She hasn't held me this close in years.

"I think about him every single day," she confides in me before she kisses the center of my forehead. "His smile, Bianca. It could melt ten feet of snow."

I step back to study her face. "I could have handled it, Mom. I could have said goodbye."

She scratches her chin. "We talked and talked about it. He didn't want you to hurt anymore. I didn't want that either."

I'm not a parent. I can't put myself in her shoes and assume I would know better.

I can only go by what Roman said to me this morning when he was leaving my apartment.

He held me close as we were tangled around each other in my bed. Our bodies were still aching from making love at dawn.

He looked me in the eyes and told me that forgiveness heals. He forgave his dad for leaving and Elizabeth for walking away from her daughters.

I had forgiven my mom before I got here.

I glance over her shoulder to see Thurston standing under a tree. I knew he would be close. He's protective of her.

He's helped her heal and grow.

He's loved her back to life.

"Did you ever go see him at Lennox Hill?" I ask. "Did you see him before he died?"

"Every morning after I took you and Vivi to school, I'd drop by." She swallows. "Often, he would be asleep, but I'd sit next to him. I wanted to be there when he passed. I hoped I would, but I couldn't get there in time."

"Roman was there."

"Roman," she repeats his name. "The man who loves you."

"The man I love," I tell her.

She nods. "He's a good man. Honest men aren't easy to find."

"I know."

"I told Vivi." She hangs her head. "I don't know if she'll come to understand why we did what we did."

I know my sister. She'll come around.

"She will, Mom."

"This guilt." Her voice breaks. "This guilt has consumed me. Every time I see you, I question whether we did the right thing."

I take both her hands in mine. "You and dad did what you thought was right at the time. You followed your hearts."

"We did," she agrees. "Regret is a difficult burden to live with."

I've seen it firsthand. That's what has kept her from letting us in. She's shrouded herself in so much guilt and regret that she's built a wall around herself.

"Let it go, Mom." I reach for her face. "Please, Mom, let it go."

A single tear falls from her cheek and onto the lapel of the light blue jacket of her pantsuit. "I'll try."

"Good."

"I'll never forget him." She leans closer to me. "I love Thurston, but your dad was the one. He was the love of my life."

"I think Roman is the love of mine."

"You'll have children?" she asks with a perk of her brows. "I'd love to be a grandmother."

I try desperately to keep my emotions at bay. "He has twin daughters. They're identical."

"Twins?" She smiles. "How old are they? What are their names?"

"They're six." I exhale. "One is named Dora, and the other is Georgie."

Her eyes stare into mine, and I see the question there, so I answer it. "Roman named her after dad."

Her hand darts to her mouth to cover a sob. "They're our family. We're going to be a family."

"I want that," I admit. "I think he does too."

Chapter 53

Roman

I watch as Bianca sits on the couch with my daughters. Georgie is cuddled into Bianca's lap. Dora is resting her head against Bianca's chest. All three of them are engrossed in a documentary about penguins.

Clearing my throat, I step closer to him. "I thought someone wanted popcorn."

Dora is the first to turn in my direction. "Come and sit with us, Daddy. We're watching this show about pen guns."

"Penguins," Georgie corrects her with a grin. "I got it right, and you got it wrong."

Bianca's hand darts out to stop the girls from yanking on each other. "Some words are harder to say than others."

"Like what?" Dora turns to look at me. "Are some words hard for you to say, Daddy?"

A couple of months ago, I thought it would be impossible to tell a woman I loved her, but I've been tossing those words at Bianca all week.

She came to my office the other day after she met with her mom at the cemetery. I held her and told her I loved her.

I did the same that night when I was making love to her in her bed.

I've repeated it at least a dozen times a day since.

"I don't know," I answer to buy some time. "Do you think I have trouble with some words?"

"You know how to say no," Georgie points out. "And how to say it's bedtime, girls."

Dora takes over. "You can say brush your teeth and put your clothes in the hamper."

Bianca chimes in, "I'd say that your dad knows how to say the New York Yankees rule, but he chooses not to."

"The Mets rule," Georgie pipes up.

"No way," Dora says, shaking her head. "It's the New York Yankees."

I catch Bianca's eye. "We will all have to agree to disagree."

The girls turn their attention back to the TV.

"This might be the best Saturday night of my life," I whisper to Bianca.

She leans closer to me. "Just wait until later, Rome."

Rome.

The nickname started years ago when George called me that. I told Matt. He picked it up, and since then, it's become a staple for the people closest to me.

Hearing Bianca say it adds another layer to it.

It feels fucking perfect.

"I can't wait, B."

Her cheeks flush.

"They're talking about kissing again," Georgie whisper shouts to her sister.

"Because they are in love," Dora stresses the last word.

"We are."

Both of my daughters turn to look at me, so I turn down the volume on the TV. "I love Bianca."

"I love your dad," she adds.

That sends both girls to their feet on the couch. They wobble and tumble on top of us.

Giggles abound as I try and hold them up so they don't roll onto the floor.

"We love Binanca too," Georgie screams. "From here to eternity."

"You said it right." Dora lunges forward to hug her sister. "You said eternity."

"I'm saying it too." I chuckle. "This right here is for eternity, B."

"For eternity," she agrees. "That sounds perfect to me."

***

I cradle Bianca against me in my bed as we both come down from the high. We made love tenderly and slowly after the girls fell asleep in their room.

"You'll stay the night."

"That doesn't sound like a question, Roman."

"It's not. I'm telling you that you're spending the night." I run a hand over her back until it's resting on her bare ass. "You want to."

"I do," she says quietly.

"Spend every night here."

That sends her back half a foot. Her eyes lock on mine. "What?"

I know she heard me, but I repeat it so there's no question. "I want you to move in with us."

Squinting, she studies my face. "We should talk to Georgie and Dora about it."

"I have," I admit. "Last night. I asked them how they felt about the idea."

"And they said?" she asks impatiently.

"They said that they want you here." I don't know if she's ready to hear what I'm about to say, but I promised her honesty, so I let it out. "They asked if you're going to be their mom."

A silent sob wrenches her body forward. "Roman."

"I know it's a hell of a lot to digest," I go on, "I'll understand if you need time, but just so you know, I want it…"

"I'll do it."

I sit up. "You'll move in?"

"My lease is up at the end of next month." She touches my chest. "I can slowly bring my things over before then."

"I'll help."

"We're really going to do this?" Her gaze flits over my face. "We're going to be a family, Rome."

"We already are." I move to kiss her. "I love you."

"I love you," she whispers.

I tug her closer and kiss her gently before I flip her over so I can show her just how much I love, want, and need her.

Epilogue

6 Months Later

Bianca

"These daisies came for you." Paige whips a beautiful bouquet of daisies from behind her back. "There's a card too. Roman is romantic, but you know that."

I do know that.

He's been sending me flowers every week. At home, he's constantly hiding chocolate bars with secret messages for me to find.

The one I discovered two days ago in the nightstand drawer was a reminder that he loves me endlessly, completely, and forever.

I kept that message as I do every single one.

Paige hands the flowers to me before she backs up. "I know the drill. Close the door on my way out."

I laugh. "Thanks, Paige."

"Thank you." She smiles. "For once again reminding me that true love may be waiting for me at a bar somewhere in this city."

Paige swooned when Vivi and I filled her in on my love story with Roman. She was in tears before I got to the part about Rome knowing my father.

It brings tears of joy to Vivi too whenever we talk about it.

"You'll find him one day, Paige."

"I believe that," she says. "It's hard to be patient, but if the payout is anything close to what you're experiencing, I'm happy to wait it out."

With a wave of her hand, she walks out of my office, shutting the door behind her.

I rip into the envelope that's tucked into the bouquet.

I smile when I read the card.

Meet me at Bow Bridge in Central Park today at 6 PM.

I glance at the screen of my phone.

"I need to hurry," I mutter to myself as I scoop up the daisies, my purse, and phone.

I take off out of my office with a smile on my face.

***

As soon as I approach the bridge, I see the man I love standing there.

He's dressed in a three-piece gray suit that matches the skirt I'm wearing. He opted for a dark blue button-down shirt this morning. I chose his tie. It's light blue with a thin thread of red running through it.

He's gorgeous.

His hand jumps into the air as he sees me nearing him.

I up my pace the same way I always do when I'm about to kiss him.

Once I'm in front of him, I grab his tie, tug him down, and plant one right on his mouth.

He groans through it. "What the fuck did I do to deserve that?"

"It's what you did last night," I whisper as people dart past us.

"You tasted like heaven." He kisses me again. "I'll get another taste tonight."

His gaze drops to the bouquet of daisies in my hand. "You brought the flowers."

"I'm going to put them in water at home."

"Home," he repeats in a low tone as he takes the flowers from me. "I'll never get tired of that. Our home, Bianca."

"Our home." I smile. "Our life."

"Our wedding."

My heart stalls for a beat. "What?"

I stare in disbelief as he drops to one knee in the middle of the bridge. People passing us slow as they near where we are.

He sets the flowers down before he tugs a small box from the inner pocket of his suit jacket. "My beautiful Bianca. I don't know how it happened, but somewhere along the way, I became the luckiest man ever to live."

My eyes swell with tears as he goes on, "I can't imagine living a day without you. I can't fathom what a future without you feels like. You are the person who knows me best and the one who holds my heart."

"Roman," I whisper. "I love you."

"Marry me," he says. "Let me love you forever."

Nodding, I almost fall forward. "Yes! Yes! I'll marry you!"

Applause erupts around us as Roman slides a beautiful silver ring on my finger.

Through falling tears, I stare at it.

He skims a finger over it as he holds me close. "That's my birthstone, our girls' birthstone, and yours is in the center."

"Our girls," I repeat.

He kisses me softly. "Our daughters."

I hear them before I see them. Dora's screams and Georgie's shriek of happiness flood me with pure joy.

I turn to see them racing toward us holding hands.

I scoop up Dora. Georgie clings to her dad.

"You're our mommy," Dora whispers as she rests her head on my shoulder. "We can call you mommy now?"

They have been on and off for weeks. I've never corrected them. Roman hasn't either.

It's who I am. It's who I always want to be.

"Yes," I answer softly. "I'd love that."

"For the wedding, can we get a gift?" Georgie asks.

"No dog until you're eight," Roman says. "I promise when you're eight, we'll adopt a dog."

"I wasn't talking about that." She swats Roman's shoulder. "We want a baby brother."

My gaze darts to Roman. His eyes widen. "We'll see what we can do."

I'm right there with him, nodding along. "We'll see."

Georgie kisses Roman's cheek. "I love our family so much."

"I love it more." Dora pumps her fist in the air.

"I love it most," Roman says.

I step closer to him so the four of us can share a big embrace. "I love you all the most."

I do.

This wonderful man and these beautiful girls have given me more than I could ever have asked for. I feel loved in a way I never imagined I would, and I love them all in a deeply profound sense that I know will only grow with each passing day.

"Let's go eat." Georgie slides down my body. "Granny Angie is waiting. She said we're going to Lise for dinner. Uncle Matty is meeting us there."

I glance up to see my mom in tears at the end of the bridge. Thurston is by her side.

They've seamlessly stepped into the roles of loving grandparents.

"You two run ahead," Roman says to our daughters. "We'll catch up."

Georgie and Dora run full force toward my mom and Thurston as Roman turns to me.

Bending down, he scoops the bouquet of daisies into his palm. "Should we let the flower decide?"

I shake my head. "Roman."

He plucks one petal. "Tell them now." He plucks another petal. "Tell them later."

My gaze falls to the front of the black sweater I'm wearing. "One more week, and we'll share the news with the girls."

His hand moves to rest on the baby bump that I've expertly kept hidden. Even Maren hasn't noticed, although she's had her hands full with her newborn son.

Last week when I met Sabrina for lunch, she told me I was glowing, but I swiftly changed the subject to the new guy she's dating. She's not sure if it will last long-term, but for the moment, she's having fun.

"The world is about to be a whole lot brighter," he says. "There's another Hawthorne on the way."

I nod.

He glances at the ring he placed on my finger. "Ivy said we could add as many stones to the band as we want, so when the baby is born, we'll take the ring in and have that done."

Ivy Marlow-Walker is the jeweler behind the masterpiece on my finger. Rome and I met her two months ago when we asked her to design bracelets for the girls to commemorate their upcoming seventh birthdays. I had no idea that Roman commissioned an engagement ring too.

He pulls me closer to him. "It is just one, right?"

I trail a finger over his chin before I kiss him. "Just one baby, Roman. Our baby."

"Our baby," he repeats. "Our family. Our fucking life. Can you believe it's this good?"

I stare into his eyes, seeing the joy in his soul and knowing that every day forward will be filled with this much love. "I believe it."

He kisses me again. It's so soft and tender that my knees weaken. "This is just the beginning, Bianca. We have a lifetime left to love each other."

"I can't wait, Roman," I whisper. "I can't wait to see what tomorrow brings."

Preview of CATCH

If you're curious about Maren's story...

What would you do if you discovered your new boss in his office with no pants, a magnum of champagne, and a glitter cannon?

Asking for a friend.

I found something that belongs to Keats Morgan, the notorious bad boy sports agent. So I do the right thing.

I return it.

You'd think the man would be happy to have it back.

He's not.

Instead, he proceeds to fire his assistant right in front of me.

He looks to me to step in as a replacement, but I want nothing to do with the jerk.

Keats is gorgeous and charming as hell. It's his arrogant attitude that makes me turn around and almost walk out the door.

The problem? I desperately need a job. Any job. And Keats is offering me an incredible one.

I agree to his terms before I realize there's a catch, and it's a big one.

Author's note: this standalone novel features a gorgeous boss and the assistant who turns his upside-down world right side up. Toss in a cute sidekick named Dudley, a trio of professional baseball players, and a twisty road to a happy ending. You're in for a swoony read with a dash of heart.

Chapter 1

Maren

"Dudley's daddy can't keep it in his pants." I flick a wrist toward my laptop screen. "I have another five DMs from women this morning."

"You have even more responses to your post on the Manhattan Lost and Found Dog group?" My roommate, Arietta Voss, comes marching into the dining room to get a better look.

I glance up and take in her outfit for the day. For a twenty-two-year-old petite blonde with gray eyes, Arietta looks nothing like you would expect her to.

The frumpy navy blue skirt wrapped around her waist hits her legs mid-calf. It's not half as bad as the lime green blouse she's buttoned up to her neck.

"You must still be beating the men off with a stick, Arietta."

She lets out a laugh. "I am trying to be professional, Maren."

"You're never going to get that sexy beast of a boss of yours in bed if you keep dressing like that."

Her eyes widen behind her dark-colored, rectangular eyeglasses. "Dominick Calvetti is still in Italy, and besides, I would never sleep with someone I hate."

"You hate him as much as I hate my vibrator," I quip.

With a shake of her head, she crosses our apartment to pull a bottle of orange juice from the fridge.

Technically, it's my apartment. If we're getting down to actual specifics, it belongs to my father. He bought this three thousand foot dream on the twentieth floor of a high rise in Tribeca as a gift for me.

It's not a standard gift, though. There are terms, and I'm already in violation of one of them.

I lost my job yesterday.

I need to stay gainfully employed to keep this lavish roof over my head.

Keeping it over Arietta's head is important to me too. We met at a vintage jewelry store a year ago. Arietta mentioned that she was looking for a place to live, and even though she's six years younger than I am, I invited her to move in.

We're as close as sisters now.

After pouring herself a glass of juice, she bends down to stroke her hand over Dudley's head. "How are you today, sweetheart?"

Arietta has been calling him that since I found him wandering the street last night without a collar.

A whole host of responses to my posting on the Manhattan Lost and Found Dog group have clued me into his name.

They also directed me toward his irresponsible owner.

Keats Morgan.

Mr. Morgan is a twenty-nine-year-old sports agent. His client list is impressive, but that's not why he's so popular in Manhattan.

Every reply to my posting about the lost dog has come from a woman.

Twenty-three women have messaged me to say that they met Dudley when they spent the night with Keats.

I push my curly red hair back behind my ears. "I sent Keats a DM on Instagram, but I got nothing back. When I called his office just now, the woman who answered the phone put me on hold and then hung up on me."

"I'd get fired if I tried that trick." Arietta bites her bottom lip. "I'm sorry. That was insensitive. I can ask at work if there are any available positions."

Arietta works as an assistant at a wealth management firm. My background is in public relations. "You're an angel, Arietta, but I'm going to put out some feelers today."

I'll do that very quietly, so my dad doesn't get wind of my employment status.

"If you know the address to Mr. Morgan's office, I can drop the dog off on my way to work," Arietta offers.

Keats Morgan is all kinds of gorgeous, and I haven't been on a date in two months. I could use a glimpse of something tall, green-eyed, and handsome today.

"I'll get dressed and head over to his office." I point at the cute dog sitting on the floor watching us. "Say your goodbyes to Dudley because he's about to be reunited with the man who can't keep him on a leash."

Read CATCH now!

THANK YOU

Thank you for purchasing and downloading my book. I can't even begin to put to words what it means to me. If you enjoyed it, please remember to write a review for it. Let me know your thoughts! I want to keep my readers happy.

For more information on new series and standalones, please visit my website, https://deborahbladon.com. There are book trailers and other goodies to check out.

If you want to chat with me personally, please LIKE my page on Facebook. I love connecting with all of my readers because without you, none of this would be possible.
www.facebook.com/authordeborahbladon

Thank you, for everything.

ABOUT THE AUTHOR

Deborah Bladon has never read a romance hero she didn't like. Her love for romance novels began when she was old enough to board the bus, library card in hand to check out the newest Harlequin paperbacks. She's a Canadian by heart, and by passport, but you can often spot her in New York City sipping a latte and looking for inspiration for her next story. Manhattan is definitely her second home.

She cherishes her family and believes that each day is a gift for writing, for reading, and for loving.

Printed in Great Britain
by Amazon

74330777R00159